DAISIES in the WILD

DAISIES in the WILD

Stuti Agarwal

HarperCollins *Publishers* India

First published in India by HarperCollins *Publishers* 2025
Cyber City, Building 10-A, Gurugram, Haryana-122002, India
www.harpercollins.co.in

2 4 6 8 10 9 7 5 3 1

Copyright © Stuti Agarwal 2025

P-ISBN: 978-93-6569-237-2
E-ISBN: 978-93-6569-744-5

This is a work of fiction and all characters and incidents described in this book are the product of the author's imagination. Any resemblance to actual persons, living or dead, is entirely coincidental.

Stuti Agarwal asserts the moral right to be identified as the author of this work.

All rights reserved. No part of this publication may be reproduced, stored in a retrieval system, or transmitted, in any form or by any means, electronic, mechanical, photocopying, recording or otherwise, without the prior permission of the publishers. Without limiting the exclusive rights of any author, contributor or the publisher of this publication, any unauthorized use of this publication to train generative artificial intelligence (AI) technologies is expressly prohibited. HarperCollins also exercise their rights under Article 4(3) of the Digital Single Market Directive 2019/790 and expressly reserve this publication from the text and data-mining exception.

Typeset in 10/14 Sabon LT Std
by HarperCollins *Publishers* India Pvt. Ltd

Printed and bound at
Replika Press Pvt. Ltd.

HarperCollins *Publishers*, Macken House, 39/40 Mayor Street Upper, Dublin 1, D01 C9W8, Ireland

This is a work of fiction. Unless otherwise indicated, all the names, characters, businesses, places, events and incidents in this book are either the product of the author's imagination or used in a fictitious manner. Any resemblance to actual persons, living or dead, or actual events is purely coincidental.

This book contains material that may be considered sexually explicit, offensive or unsettling to some readers. Specifically, it includes explicit language and adult themes, e.g. sexual content, underage same-sex relationships, student-teacher romantic involvements, etc.

This book explores mature themes and sensitive topics purely for artistic and creative purposes. It aims to foster understanding, empathy, and is in the interest of the cause of literature, while adhering to the boundaries of constitutional rights, cultural sensitivities and applicable Indian law. The content is not intended to offend, defame or contravene any legal, moral or societal norms, nor hurt any religious sentiments. Readers are encouraged to engage with the material responsibly and respectfully within the context of its intent.

Foreword

I don't remember ever being far away from books. They've always been friends who have had my back—friends I have laughed with, friends who have shared a cry, friends I have greatly learnt from. Often, they've been my recourse through tough times and difficult decisions. I suppose it is easier to accept, even absorb lessons hidden in pages of faraway fiction than when spelled out by near and dear ones. As a mother now, it's a conundrum I am learning to find my way through—how much do we teach and how much we leave them to learn—a perilous parenting maze that so many of us flounder in while we attempt to do the best for our children. But what is it they say about good intentions?! The road to hell is paved with them. We always mean well, but the consequences of our actions are not always good. And it is while I deal with this rather perplexing dilemma that I've found a ray of light in Stuti's *Daisies in the Wild*, one that led me back to the belief that perhaps the right piece of fiction can offer the answers we are hoping our children, even we as adults, find.

The story of Ina, Nidra, and Pema, inspired by Stuti's childhood home in Darjeeling and her days in a boarding school is one of friendship, love and identity—an honest exploration of the teen years in the midst of conflict, both internal and external. How often have we felt the upheaval between what we earnestly wish for and what we are told by those around us we should want? How often have we been confronted by the conflict of heart and mind, and that battle with the status quo, even societal standards? I've seen some find the courage to accept themselves, chase their heart, fight that war against others and pursue their happiness. Sometimes those who do are those we least expect it from. I also know of so many who make a heartbreaking choice to let go of a part of themselves—sometimes their very being, sometimes little bits that add up to a whole lot—keep it hidden because the fight is so very hard.

It's impossible to be everything to everyone. Shouldn't we then might as well start by being true to ourselves first? After all, it's who we'll have through all the years no matter what. This has been at the core of my learnings over the many years, and it's been something that has been integral to my parenting over the last seven. I have new anxieties and worries every day, but a consistent one is ensuring my daughter's happiness. As much as I want to shield her, fight her battles, be her wings, I know I need to step away and empower her to be brave and fight her own battles, the ones she truly cares for. I want her to be not what I imagine she can be but who she chooses to be. I need to talk less and listen more, and be the silent wind beneath her wings, pushing her to fly on and high.

In this mix, perhaps I will leave precious books lying around her room, and this one is going to be one of them. I hope she discovers in these pages the wisdom, gentleness, and courage of Ina; I wish she learns from Pema the importance of looking within to correct what is outside and the need to be gentle with oneself; and I hope she finds with Nidra what it is to really let go and have fun. But, most of all, I hope by the end of it she finds lifelong friends who help her find the fierce ability to be herself—I know, even today, reading this book was a nudge towards that rediscovery, one I also hope fellow teachers and parents can embrace. This may be one you wouldn't want to miss.

Lots of love,
Soha Ali Khan

Note from the Author

I love the idea of an overworked notebook—one filled with different inks and hands, hurried notes and almost inscrutable scribbles, so many that they're forgotten over the years. I have one with me all the time, no matter what. No phone has been able to replace these pages, and while many mundane an idea has been born and forgotten in them, there were two that I witnessed for myself that have haunted me for seventeen long years.

The first, and more a catalyst than the story in these pages itself, is that of the fight for Gorkhaland. Over the years, I've read plenty novels about the many political fractions in the country, and not enough about the demand for separate statehood that has gripped my hometown, the Darjeeling district, for decades—affecting its economy, education, heritage, and social fabric forever. No, that's been limited to local newspapers and a handful of non-fiction and research papers that I ransacked town libraries for as I started work on *Daisies in the Wild*. Yet, as someone who has been born and brought up in the town and seen the agitation escalate over the years to the severe riots and strikes of 2017, it has been a conversation that has simmered for as long as I can remember in my home and mind, sometimes loud, sometimes in scared whispers, changing our lives in ways that have been comprehensible only in hindsight, beginning with me having to leave for a boarding school in Dehradun.

Which brings me to the next part of my story, the flesh and bone of it in a lot of ways, a story I was as much a witness to as a part of—that of three teenage girls who found friendship, family and adventure with each other; discovered themselves and fought their ascribed vs acquired identities; came together and fell apart on the sprawling campus of a boarding school. It is also a love story between two of them, and the discovery of love and sexuality at a young age.

The story I tell is a fictionalized one, yet it is as real a story as I have ever written. It is a dialogue on a political battle that has wrenched the life out of a peaceful hill town for decades. It is also a reflection on the homophobia that underlies Indian society, how people live with it, and the love that blossoms despite it. And ultimately, it is a desperate attempt to understand how we can heal from the scars that are left on us early on to become who *we* want to be.

Dear readers, the story in these pages has come together over a decade of research, notes-taking, interviews, readings of my cringey diaries as a teenager and fourteen drafts. I hope you will turn the pages with gentleness, offer Pema, Nidra and Ina an open mind and heart, and let them be a part of your lives in all their damaged glory.

Praise for *Daisies in the Wild*

'A gentle and sensitive portrayal of coming-of-age friendship, faith, love, and conflict, both around us and within. There could not be a better time for this story. A must read for parents and teenagers alike.'

**Aniruddha Roy Chowdhary,
National Award-Winning Film Director**

'This book beautifully captures the unfiltered chaos of adolescence—the longing for belonging, the quiet rebellions, and the friendships that shape us. It's raw, honest, and deeply relatable.'

**Masoom Minawala, Global Fashion Influencer,
Entrepreneur and Author**

'The social and political status of every society plays a vital role in the way it helps shape our present and the future. The Gorkhaland agitation is certainly one of them. I have been witness to when it all started in 1986. I was an eighth standard student in one of the boarding schools in Kurseong, and what came as a blessing for more playtime (because of the strikes) became a critical reason for the way the hills have changed for the worse over the last three decades.

While all of us would have had our own experiences with it, not many may have the will to pen it down as beautifully as Stuti Agarwal has done. Life throws all sort of challenges to each one of us, but it is the bonds we share in friendship that help us overcome them and evolve as mindful beings in the course of our lives. The story of Inayat, Pema, and Nidra's friendship is certainly the story of many such young people, who face socio-political challenges even today in different parts of the world.

I congratulate Stuti for writing this fantastic book and I am confident that this story will in some form help bring about a positive change in the hills of Darjeeling and the global society as a whole. My best wishes for the success of this book.'

Yangdup Lama,
Mixologist, Entrepreneur and Mentor

'Stuti's *Daisies in the Wild* is a true gem that transports you straight into the heart of Darjeeling, capturing the complex dance of adolescence with grace and honesty. As you wander through its pages, you'll find yourself entwined in the lives of characters who are as real as they are enchanting, each struggling to find their place in the world. It's a journey through the bittersweet trials of youth, filled with moments that will make you laugh, pause, and maybe even tear up a bit. It's the kind of book that sticks with you, like a conversation with an old friend beneath the shaded trees of a familiar schoolyard.'

Anwesh Sahoo,
Visual Designer and Technical Artist

'Stuti has found a way to talk about taboo and difficult issues confronting young AFABs in India, with a flair of mischief and youthful excitement. An important book which makes us question our society, reality and threshold of what is considered acceptable.'

Durga Shakti Gawde,
Artist, Activist, India's 1st drag king and drag dominatrix

'This book is a precious insight into the turbulent times we lived through during the Gorkhaland agitation. It brings back memories of my life and what it did to so many like me. Stuti Agarwal's work is definitely one that takes readers to a journey into the lives of not just the three protagonists but into the lives of thousands of people of the Darjeeling hills whose life changed forever. A fabulous read, this book that touched my heart.'

Doma Wang,
Chef and Entrepreneur, The Blue Poppy Restaurants

'*Daisies in the Wild* is a brave, unflinching exploration of teenage identity and the beliefs that shape us—those we inherit and those we discover on our own. Stuti's writing opens up conversations that are often silenced, offering a safe space for reflection and growth. In Ina, Nidra, and Pema, I found more than characters—I found mirrors of my own journey and a reminder of the resilience it takes to come of age. This book doesn't just tell a story; it heals. Thank you, Stuti, for the courage and care woven into every page.'

Keshav Suri,
Executive Director, The Lalit Suri Hospitality Group
& Founder, Keshav Suri Foundation

'Stuti's *Daisies in the Wild* is a gentle and thoughtful exploration of the familiar adolescent struggles of love, friendship, identity and societal understanding. Through it I found friends in Ina, Nidra and Pema, who left me wishing I had found both them and the book earlier, as I traversed my own battles.'

Shivesh Bhatia,
Baker and Author of Best-selling Cookbooks

To Smit, without whom this book would have never happened

Sarah, for giving me Ina and the many contradictions

Shivek, for being the undeterred cheerleader every writer deserves

Duhin, who read it first and said 'umm'

Arshia, who helped me heal my Pema

Tanvi, the silent support I never asked for but desperately needed

Hunar and Vani, who let me live 16 in 2017

And my family, for putting up with my limited self and never letting me go hungry

CHAPTER 1

PEMA

I could tell she didn't want to be there. She had that anywhere-but-here look that I would totally wear around the school if I could. Not judgy or anything, but like disappointed as hell maybe, even sad. I couldn't exactly figure what it was, but it looked like she was dying to run away or something. And, I mean, like who could blame her. Five years later and I still feel that way about St Mary's. Honestly, if I wasn't trying so hard to be liked, I'd have this anywhere-but-here look that would be 10 per cent disappointment, 15 per cent sadness, 20 per cent boredom, 25 per cent pure hatred, maybe about 30 per cent jealousy and like an extra 5 per cent of cringe and cranks thrown in like Domino's oregano or something, but with extra of that garlic. And I'm only a day scholar, which means I am out of here by 3:30 p.m., 5:30 max on days there is some kind of practice, which does happen often actually. Of course, being a day scholar probably is a big reason for my hatred for the place; that and the nuns who have this annoying thing about turning us into 'ladies', whatever that even means. Although they also have these long masses—really huge-ass productions of sorts that the whole school has to be part of, with choir practice and stuff, which can be really exhausting, but that is a story for another time. I was saying ... oh ya, St Mary's. God, just the name makes me want to throw up. But also, now that I think about it, I don't understand why like families send their kids to boarding schools far away from themselves, all the way to Darjeeling in St Mary's case. Maybe parents want to get rid of their annoying kids, straighten them out and whatnot (I mean, I've watched *Udaan* and *Taare Zameen Par* and *Warrior High*, so I know what parents think will happen in boarding schools. Of course, you're hoping for an Ishaan and not Rohan. Even the whole Poppy Moore transformation in *Wild Child* could work I suppose). But none of them seem like her at all. Anyways, it isn't like I have any real friends in this school to base all this grand theory on (probably the shittiest thing about my life might I add). For all I know people actually believe that it could be great for their like angelic kids or something. Wait, but that wasn't what I was talking about. Seriously, I get distracted way too easily, but I'm kind of working on it so I guess it's kind of okay.

Oh ya, I was saying, I can't imagine what it would be like for her. I mean, she's come in weeks after term started, plus in the tenth grade. No one ever comes in the tenth or twelfth grade, like it doesn't make sense with the board exams and stuff, which makes me wonder why she's here. From all the gossip I have eavesheard … is 'eavesheard' a thing? I think it should be. Anyways, from all the gossip I've eavesheard over the years, I want to guess it is because something life-altering happened, maybe even like tragic AF or something. I'll probably ask her when we become friends. Obviously I knew as soon as she walked into class that we'd be friends, for a while anyways (which kind of always is the case with me). Mainly because she was going to need one—people here can get quite cliquey, especially with newcomers (unless, I guess if a Bollywood nepo baby showed up tomorrow spilling insider secrets about nose and boob jobs and dating histories or something)—and, because I don't really have any, I'm not all that picky. In fact, I am going to try my hardest before she somehow becomes friends with the others, which also always happens after a bit.

Now I feel like I should explain why I have no real friends when I've been here for so long before I come across as some sort of total psycho. Like, I'm not evil or anything as the nuns call it. But I am a day scholar, which means that while I'm part of everyday chats about which new Wattpad story is about Harry Styles, the latest Marvel and One Direction releases, whether Bieber and Selena are back again, or a debate of TWICE vs. EXO vs. Red Velvet, I'm not really *actually* part of the groups. I mean, you get it. I guess there is a lot I miss once I go home and, somehow, it's never the same no matter how hard I try. Plus, there's the whole the cliché that I *am* a teacher's daughter. Baba teaches physics at St Mary's and there is always the 'she'll go tell her father' thing. Like, there have been so many times when the girls were busy gossiping about teachers and other girls and their boyfriends, making late night plans of tuck raids and parties, and have quickly shut up or pretended to talk about something else when they saw me. But I guess at least they're always sweet to me because of it, and I do have a few class friends type situations that aren't all bad—like Shefali, and Charu, Aabha, even Shivangi to a certain extent. I once tried blackmailing my parents into letting me become a boarder, I am pretty sure that is the solution for most of my problems (my looks I can't do anything about myself really), but they said they didn't have the money for the boarding fees and that was that.

'Hi ... umm ... is it okay if I sit here?' she whispered as she walked to my desk.

You don't really have a choice, do you? All other desks are taken. I shushed my mind. It has this habit of being super negative about everything and jumping to just like awful assumptions all the time. Aama says I must train it not to.

'Ya, sure,' I smiled instead, 'I'm Pema.'

'Inayat,' she gave a quick smile before sitting down to unpack her bag into the desk, arranging her books into proper piles, not like my messy dump.

Neat freak, my mind said. I shushed it again.

She looks shy as hell, Inayat does. Maybe it's because she's like so tiny. Or maybe because her short hair falls all over her big glasses, almost hiding her face, even though she has these huge eyes and her gold nose ring shines against her crazy white face. But it feels like she prefers it like that, like she is trying hard to stay as invisible as possible.

I watched her pile her books on one side, her notebooks on the other. The short English novels she kept in the middle along with an old wooden case for her pens.

'That's a cute box,' I tried chatting.

'It's my Nana's ... my Nani painted the prairie daisies on it,' she mumbled, looking down at the box. Her eyes began tearing up, and she quickly distracted herself with her desk again.

Looks like she misses her grandparents, I thought. *And I guess she likes these prayer daisies. Maybe I can show her the tiny daisies that grow in Darj someday, she might like that. They look pretty much the same as her box ones to me. I love the ones we have. They're so cute and friendly, like they're always giggling or something, like they're all best friends having fun. And we could even play the yes-or-no game with them, you know the one where you ask a question and then pluck each tiny petal for a yes or no until the last one left and that is god's answer or something.*

Ya ya, I know, I am getting distracted again.

She kept a letter-writing pad in front and of course I wondered about who she'd be writing to. *Maybe she has a lot of friends back home, even a boyfriend. She wouldn't need you then, would she?* My mind piped up again. *She'll use you like the others—just to chat with a little in class, get favours outside of school, and then forget about you when she's made other friends in the hostel.*

She stuck a few photos of ...

'Are ... are these your grandparents?'

She nodded.

... and a calendar of the first term with a drawing of a house at the end.

I smiled and opened my desk to show her my term calendar, the days gone struck out on it with ginormous red Xs. She looked at me and gave another small smile, and I could totally tell then that we both felt the same way about being in this school—basically not wanting to be here. I'm kind of psychic like that.

Aama lectures me a lot about how I've got to be more grateful that I get to study in such a 'great' school thanks to Baba. Each grade in

St Mary's has only about twenty-five girls, something about quality education and individual attention and whatnot. Although the only one really making the most of this is Sir Thapa, and not for the right reasons from what I've heard, if you know what I mean. And Apeksha from Grade 12 along with him might I add, for this year anyways, it changes quickly with him. Not like Sir Rai and Alisha, that love story's been going on for a while now I think. If only Aama found out about all this. She would probably throw a fit and get me out of there ASAP, but I doubt she'll ever believe me even if I told her.

Anyways, there goes my mind again. I was saying ... Aama. Ya, every time I complain she reminds me about how great the teachers are, how our principal, Sister Teresa, is one of the most learned nuns she knows and how this school will help me achieve all my dreams and stuff. (Although, I mean, I don't even have like big dreams or anything. They practically change every day—like my latest is to be a private chef with a specialization in pets, which I'm pretty sure isn't a realistic vision, especially studying here) And, like, I *am* really grateful for a lot in my life. I am grateful as hell for my father, my mother, even my brother whom I spend every summer fighting with when he comes back home from college. I am grateful for where I live and, of course, for all the books and fried food. I'm grateful for the bowl of change my mum keeps in her drawer and that she never remembers how many coins are in there. I just don't care about this school. Honestly, *any* other day school in town would do (and, side note, any improvement in how I look would really help).

Every morning I hear girls in my gao calling out to each other on their way to school, making plans, and I hate that I have to go to St Mary's. No going for afterschool momo and piro aloo for me. No one to ask me to hurry up because they couldn't leave without me. No one to walk home with while we stuff our faces with Wai Wai (even though I don't love it, unless it is Akbare). Sometimes I really hate these girls, especially when they talk about all the things that happened in their schools and the stuff they did after and how they got caught when sneaking out of school to have a momo date with their boyfriends and whatnot when we go for tuitions. Ya, I know, tell

Aama about the irony or whatever. You would think going to one of the 'best' schools in the country would mean no tuitions. But Aama doesn't like that argument, or any argument against St Mary's really. I think part of her love for St Mary's comes from the concession fee that Baba gets for me. So, anyways, looks like I am stuck here. I really do hate this like half-assed life.

'We don't have classes today?' I heard Inayat whisper.

'Oh ya, no we don't. The sport tournaments for the inter-house competition started today and a lot of the students and staff are busy there. The tenth and twelfth graders who aren't participating are supposed to 'self-study' or whatever. It goes on for three days, so we'll start full classes by Monday, but the evenings will still be packed with like cultural practices and stuff until the final performances in two weeks. You'll meet your house captain soon I'm guessing, once they're back from the field. She'll tell you everything.'

'Okay,' she nodded, turning her attention to a newly started P.G. Wodehouse.

'Hey, I've been meaning to read Wodehouse. My Baba loves him. Even Sister Stephanie, I mean our librarian, said it would be better for me or whatever. She really hated the Roald Dahl I was reading.'

'It was the country stories one,' I continued, trying really hard to have a conversation. 'I'm forgetting the name.'

'*Sweet Mystery of Life?*' she asked.

'That one! Have you read it?'

'No, my mother said it wasn't appropriate.'

'All the animal sex and slaughter, huh?'

She gave a short chuckle.

'And maggots and rat infestations,' I remembered.

'To be fair, like, *that* has got to be age appropriate as hell. But I guess I get it. But also, I mean, I had so much fun reading it! I haven't been able to finish any other book since. Baba also has *Switch Bitch* in his study. I am trying to steal it. Apparently, that has like legit sex stuff. Have you ever read or seen *Fifty Shades of Grey*? Mummy had the CD for it and I watched a little bit when my parents were away, and it was like crazy. Although, if you ask the girls, they'll probably choose *13 Reasons Why* or even *Riverdale*. I've heard some of them even masturbate to scenes from *Game of Thrones* and *Orange is the New Black*, but I haven't watched those yet.'

She didn't say anything, and I got scared that I'd made her uncomfortable. For god's sake it isn't even like I am sex-obsessed or anything. I just have got to stop blabbering like this. So I tried to change the topic. 'Would you recommend I read P.G. Wodehouse too?'

'His Jeeves collection is great. *Carry On, Jeeves*.'

'Done! I shall pick that one then.'

She smiled and went back to her book.

'You know what house you are in?' I interjected again.

'Blue.'

'No ways! I'm in Sapphire too,' I said, my mind jumping at my luck. 'You'll like Nidra, she's our house captain. She's pretty cool and not annoying like the other captains who are only chill for their friends. Actually, she said she'd meet us in the house and tell us how we did today. Wait. Hey Shef, do you know if the games are done for the day?'

Shefali is one of the class friends-ish I was talking about earlier. I've learned over time that these girls aren't actually my friends, not if I stop exchanging notes with their boyfriends for them or sneaking them some tuck now and then, but Shefali is pretty chill, and we've often been paired for assignments together. She's been in St Mary's since the fifth grade, like me, and we were both mess vice captains last year, but she is hoping to become head girl next year and so is quite busy trying to win everyone over and take charge of everything, and the way she is doing it is honestly a bit much pushy even for me.

'Oh yes, a while back I think.'

'Cool, thanks!' I turned to Inayat. 'Let's go there now? I'll have to go home after.'

'You don't live here?' she asked.

I thought it might be better not to starting cribbing just yet and give her like the *Reader's Digest* version of my story for now, as Lorelai says (you get the *Gilmore Girls* reference? I know it's an old show and stuff, but love!). Sorry, getting distracted again. I replied, 'No, my dad's a teacher here, so I have to go back with him.'

'Oh,' she said, with no change of expression to make me feel like just maybe she would have liked it if I stayed.

'Shall we go then?' I asked instead, shaking the thought off.

She nodded.

'I'm guessing you've been to the house and stuff?'

'In the morning with the matron, Miss Farzana.'

I guess now is as good a time as any to give a tour of St Mary's. Let's begin with like the basics. It is a 183-year-old British school in Darjeeling, which means it's quirky as hell, like any heritage building in a snooze fest of a town in the mountains. For starters, the entire school is like this crazy giant maze (think *Harry Potter* but less spooky castle and more Victorian palace or something. I don't know, I hope I am doing a decent job of explaining this). It is all grey stone that never needs repair other than all the moss and ivy that makes it look all gloomy, which I kind of love. Although the wooden floorboards and windowpanes are annoyingly creaky and loud, and the nuns refuse to get actual repairs because you can't have new things done to a heritage building or whatever. And because it is so ginormous and the staff can't really watch everywhere, you can have like crazy adventures, with hidden rooms, restricted areas, supposed ghosts and other stuff. I mean, *I* haven't done any of this if it wasn't obvious already from all my complaining, but I have like amazing hearing and manage to pick up on the girls talking about sneaking into the mess for a midnight snack, parties by the pool, or scaring Mrs John and her husband late at night with ghostly pranks. Fuck, I really wish I was part of all this stuff. What I wouldn't give to eat half-cooked Maggi by the pool or Parle-G with some watery hot chocolate. Sounds fucking amaze. Ugh. Whatever.

Coming back to the school tour. Let's just go one block at a time, although why I'm talking about this I don't know. It's not like it's relevant to the story or anything, but I like it when you can imagine things when you read, so that.

Right, okay, you enter the school's ridiculously large iron gates (it's like three six-feet men stacked one on top of another, maybe four) and walk down a gravelled path with these tall pine trees on both sides, which brings you to the church and administrative block. On the right is a nice garden where we sometimes have classes, but that's really only to impress the parents, because we only have these when they are visiting and also are given like really long instructions about looking cheerful, being ladylike and whatnot. Yup, ladylike is one of the many things we just *have* to be at St Mary's (elbows off the dining table, always keep your legs closed, don't laugh loudly, don't do anything loudly at all, make sure you sneeze in a whisper, don't slouch, always carry a handkerchief ... I could go on and on). Although, of course they all easily forget about it when they lift our skirts to check if we are wearing bloomers (I mean, add inappropriate much!) and smack us with a ruler on our bums (inappropriate times two!), in case we fail to wear them.

Oh my god, okay, I have to stop being confusing with this.

I was saying, once again, you keep walking ahead and you reach the classes. The residential blocks are a little far away—down from the classes, across the game grounds, further down from the mess, the kitchen garden (one of the seven school gardens) and the glasshouse—and divided into four blocks that stand in the four corners of a square. Each one represents a house—Ruby, Emerald, Diamond and Sapphire—and each house has four floors, one for two classes each. Oh, and St Mary's starts from the fifth grade. I would tell you about like the amazing life I had in a local school before I came here—that's where I made friends with Tenzing and Dawa who I go for tuitions with, although now they are so busy yapping about their school and new boyfriends that I might as well go alone—but I am trying really hard to concentrate. Right, four floors, eight classes, and the ground floor has the foyer, the common room, the infirmary, the matron's room and the laundry.

Phew. I mean, I could go on, but this should work for now before I get any more confusing and completely lose the point of the story. Oh, I should mention though, since I was talking about imagination and whatnot, that you can see the Kanchenjunga range from every part of the school, like all the time. I mean, all the time when it is sunny, which in Darjeeling isn't all that often. It's quite like that town where the Cullens live in *Twilight*; what was the name? Never mind, I wasn't much of a fan of the book anyways; something about falling in love with vampires and wolves that isn't my thing at all, even though the girls seem to love it. They've all been obsessed with *The Vampire Diaries* these days and I heard they even had a goodbye party for the last episode recently, which, okay, I totally would have wanted to be part of, even if I had to watch the whole season with them through the night.

Okay, stopping now.

Back to Inayat and me heading to the house.

We walked up the steps of the house and to the foyer, which was already packed with loud, excited girls.

'Hi Nupur. Hi Vrinda.' I waved to a few girls around.

'Aaaaa Pema, I won! I won!' Charu hugged me, making me feel pretty special. 'My treat at Dekeva's the next town outing.'

I smiled. Charu and I have been pretty chill of late. With Shef busy with god knows what and whatnot, we've been doing most of the projects together. We've even hung out together during some fruit breaks, and she's never asked me to deliver a letter or get her tuck, ever.

'You did? Amazing! I knew you could totally beat Kritika in that high jump.'

'Ya! See you in there,' she pushed her way into loud cheers.

'That's Nidra,' I said, pointing her out as we found some space to squish into. 'The school thinks that the students of the tenth and twelfth grade should be focusing on their board exams, so captains are chosen from the eleventh and the vice captains from ninth.'

'Oh,' Inayat muttered. The girl was hardly saying anything, but to be fair, it *was* her first day.

'I know, totally weird.'

'Okay, ladies. Let's do this,' Nidra announced, breaking my train of thought, as if I really needed that.

Nidra always manages to get attention. I mean, she's beautiful as hell—tall, dark, glassy skin that could make Koreans jealous, long curly hair, and this always perfect uniform. I mean, the St Mary's uniform is pretty basic—skirt, shirt, tie, blazer and knee-length socks—but Nidra makes so much grey look like super chic and kind of hot, unlike some girls who are quite into the hip-hop style with their skirt hanging just above their ankles, baggy shirts with folded sleeves and loose ties. But, more than all that, it is her confidence that's like insane—her voice, how she's always cheerful, and the way she manages to do everything and be like ridiculously good at it and still have so much fun. Basically, she's totally cool.

'Today was pretty good for us. We have a solid second position, and if we can maintain that for the next two days we should be able to take the lead with the other competitions ...'

Nidra went on super excitedly, telling everyone about the plans for the rest of the fest. 'Also, we need more hands for the play production. The sets are taking an insane amount of time. Any volunteers?'

I pushed both Inayat and my hands up, still quite excited from the conversation with Charu and the general house spirit.

'Great, Pema,' Nidra said.

Meanwhile, Inayat looked at me with ... what was it ... shock, irritation, anger, all in one neat package (I *am* going quite Lorelai Gilmore with this narration, love it!)? I couldn't tell, but give me a few days to get her.

'It might be nice for you to get to know everyone,' I whispered. *Get to know you, you mean*, my mind chimed in.

'And you are?' Nidra asked.

'Inayat,' she said softly.

I waited for her to say more, but when she didn't, I added, 'She's new in our grade.'

'Oh! Welcome to St Mary's, Inayat,' Nidra said chirpily, 'and welcome to Sapphire House. You're going to have a lot of fun, I promise.'

Inayat gave a half-assed smile, although I did wonder if it looked a little hopeful, as if Nidra had already done what I wanted to. *Jealous much?* my mind popped up again.

CHAPTER 2

NIDRA

The annual fest is probably my favourite time of the year. The entire school is just happier of sorts in those weeks, even though it is one of the gloomiest months in Darjeeling. May is when the irregular rains from the last few months turn heavier, and a thick fog hangs around the whole day. And even in the middle of this, the energy in the school is really something else. Everyone is running around from class to practice and back, and there is this crazy excitement about winning the house cup. Really, it's ... what's the phrase Miss Pradhan uses ... oh ya, happy hormones! Not gonna lie, I guess it used to be more fun when I was not captain and didn't have to worry about every detail of the fest and could focus only on the dance competition. But I can't really complain, not yet anyways, not when I literally chose this. Of course, if we lose, my friends better be ready with ridiculous amounts of junk for the long night of sulking they'll be in for. I wonder if we can get the juniors to cough up a few packets of their Wai Wai since I'm sure we'll have all finished our ration of it during prep.

Anyways, I'm still not complaining or whatever, but I'm so tired all the time these days, running from one practice to another, making sure everything is on track. Which is why I like to go down for some alone time after dinner to my favourite part of the school—the graveyard.

I know that sounds dark okay, but it's really not. The graveyard is really this insanely beautiful maze of trees with just a few graves in between them. There are rhododendrons, maple, chestnut, pines and so many others I don't know of, all huddled together in a canopy (not talking about the short wild grass though, that gets super mushy in the rains and is quite disgusting actually), with an insane view of the town on one side and the mountain range on the other—as if the nuns said 'this view would be amazing after we died'. And, added bonus, it is the shortest route to the school garden with the lake where I often sneak off for a swim with the tadpoles and fishies. The school is crazy big, so there are plenty places to go for some quiet time, but nothing beats this one, I swear.

Sister Anne Mary's grave is my favourite. She has the best view. If ghosts couldn't travel but just stand on their graves or something, then the other nuns would probably have to peek over Sister Anne Mary's shoulders for a view. And fair I guess, she *is* the founder of the school.

It has easily become the calmest time of the day for me. Just sitting there helps ...

'Ex-excuse ... umm ... excuse me ... who ... who,' I stuttered.

For all the courage I show when my friends complain of hearing ghosts in our dorms and stuff, seeing someone *actually* sitting on the grave did spook me out gonna be honest ... for only a minute though I have to add.

The person turned around.

'Hey ... hi.'

'Oh. You're ...'

'Inayat.'

'Oh ya!' I exclaimed, sighing in relief. 'You're in my house. Pema's friend, right?'

'Yes,' she murmured. 'Sorry ... I was just ... I'll go back.'

I found my way around the graves to her. Despite the fog, there was enough moonlight for me to see that she'd been crying, basic newcomer stuff.

'That's cool. I was just a little surprised. I've never seen anyone here before,' I said, trying not to make her feel uncomfortable.

'I just ... I wanted to be alone.'

'Ya, I know the feeling,' I gave her an empathetic smile and sat down on the grave next to her.

She sat quietly, looking away, a crumbled paper—a letter maybe—in her hands, biting her lip to kinda stop herself from crying again.

'So, how did you find this place?' I asked, not wanting to mess with whatever was bothering her.

'I was just taking a stroll down from the dorms.'

I knew it wasn't that simple. The graveyard wasn't a place you just found. It could only be found if you kinda *really* wanted to, you know; the school had made sure of that with the tall ivy hedges around it. And who in their right mind would make their way through that and into the forest, even if it was a friendly one like this? Sure, girls tried to dare each other to come here in the day, but hardly anyone tried it at night, and definitely never alone. There were more than enough stories to keep you away. Nope, the graveyard had to really be sought out or whatever. Not to make it sound like the Room of Requirement or anything, although it would be pretty cool if there ever were one. Every time we have a weekend *Harry Potter* marathon, there is always someone or the other who asks what we would want from all the *Harry Potter* movies IRL and it's the only thing I want, ever. I mean, think about it, the room gives you everything you want or need, so, realistically, why would you want anything else?

I suppose then she *was* seeking it.

'And how has your week in the school been so far? Are you having fun?'

She shrugged, getting teary again, so I thought I'd let her be. 'The first few weeks are tough on everyone, but you'll settle in. I remember my first term. I did nothing but cry and write my mom letters about how awful the school is—the cold showers we had to take in the mornings, the lice in the girls' hair, the lunatic matron, games in the morning AND night, having to figure my laundry, the bad food and very little snacks and whatnot—begging her to come take me back. Keep yourself busy with the production, that will help.'

I could tell she was holding back crying, like really crying, and I wasn't sure I could handle that.

'And, I'm just a floor above yours. You can always come hang out with me,' I tried cheering her up. We are never up to great stuff, but it's fun. Like the other day, we glued all the laundry bags shut so we wouldn't have to do our laundry! Miss Farzana was so mad.'

She smiled.

I reached for her hand and gave it a little squeeze. 'I know it must be hard, coming between term and being the only new girl in your grade. St Mary's can get pretty cliquey that way. And I'm sure you're not happy about being here and leaving your old life behind, I know I wasn't. But as someone who felt the same, I'll tell you this—give this place a chance, it could surprise you. It could be your home away from home. I'll try and help if you want. How about tomorrow? We're planning on raiding the mess pantry for some tuck. We're all dead with the fest work and our stock is almost over. Why don't you come?'

'Okay,' she mumbled.

We sat there for a long while, not saying anything. I guess we both really needed some quiet time. Of course, she needed it for much longer than I did. What can I say, I like having a heart-to-heart with Sister Anne Mary after a bit. But it felt kinda okay actually, not like when I am with my friends and any silence has to be filled with some stupid hypothesis or gossip.

It was only when my watch beeped that I realized we had stayed way past bedtime!

'Fuck, we better go. Miss Farzana will be doing her rounds soon, and we really must be back before that. Plus, I *am* the house captain, imagine me getting caught!'

We got up and ran out of the graveyard, up another school garden, across the altar and the herb glasshouse and into the residential block.

'This way, Miss Farzana will almost be done watching *Naagin* in the common room. We should go through here,' I whispered, taking her hand and leading her to the laundry room window.

'I think the TV just got shut off,' Inayat said.

'Oh fuck, okay,' I said. 'We really need to rush.'

I helped her up and we crept across the laundry room to our dorms.

'See you tomorrow,' I said.

'See you,' Inayat smiled hesitantly.

CHAPTER 3

INAYAT

Dear God,

 I miss Nani Nana. I got their letter today, and I know they were trying to cheer me up, telling me about the goings on in Jubilee Hills, Nani's latest batch of olive czochworu and the new menu at the club. Still, all I could think of was life before Ammi decided to skip off to Lucknow to live with her new husband. I keep replaying the night she told us about her decision. It all feels so fresh in my head. How I begged her to let me stay in Hyderabad, promising her I could help Nani at home and with Nana's health; how I overheard Nani pleading her to let me stay. But Ammi didn't listen, did she? You didn't want her to. I cannot stop replaying those days in my mind every minute I get alone, sometimes even when I'm surrounded by people.

 Why didn't Ammi listen? Why did I have to come here? Why did you take Nani Nana away from me? First Abba and now them?

 I miss our Thursday night dinners at the club, and weekend pool sessions with Nana. I miss spending time with Nani in the kitchen, helping her prep the vegetables for her pickles, her watching over my back as Sidra Di and I made keema parathas for everyone. I miss gardening with Nana, even though he pulled my ear for every weed I left. I miss hanging the laundry out in the garden with Nani while Nana sat reading on the veranda in his rocking chair. I miss grinding mehndi leaves on the sill for Nani to put on her and Sidra Di's hands every week. I miss doing sudoku puzzles with Nana and secretly letting him have my biscuits and sweet tea.

I had finally started to feel happy after Ammi left Abba and moved us to Hyderabad. I had found family in Nani Nana and Sidra Di, discovered pottery. Why this then? Why give me all that to take it away again? It might have been easier if it had never gotten better. I can't seem to make sense of any of it.

Nani tells me that I must never forget that you are looking out for me, that this is all a test and I will understand your will in time, even come to cherish it, but why do I have to be tested at all? I've been a nice person, haven't I? Is it because I don't pray all my salahs of the day? I try to. But Nani always says that you're my friend, that if I'm an honest person you'll take care of me. But if you are a friend, then why would you put me through my version of Kafka?

Nani also says I must be patient. I suppose that is one thing I'm not, but I promise this time I will try to be. You showed me a path when we moved to Hyderabad, and I will write to you every night and pray that I find that here, too.

I suppose, while I do that, I should thank you for Pema. She has really helped me get around the school in the last few days. She is always there, and she talks a lot, which I like because it helps me drown out everything going on in my mind, even though she can often get forceful with her inquiries. But she leaves after lunch, and the voices in my head return, and the rest of the day is terribly difficult.

Although, tonight wasn't. It's strange, how I felt with Nidra. Everyone around me seems to love her, and I can understand why—she is fun, friendly, and perhaps the most beautiful girl I've ever seen in real life—but it wasn't any of that. I think it was that she didn't prod me with inquisitions or look at me with sympathy. But, more than any of that, for the first time since I've been here, I felt comforted, like I could breathe again without worrying about being reminded of the past. And when she held my hand and told me it was going to be okay, my heart wanted to believe her, like it did Nani when she whispered it in my ears as I was leaving. I cannot explain why I felt like that. I don't know her at all to feel at ease with her. In fact, I don't know if

I ought to feel any sense of solace with her, but I must thank you for it, even though it may as well be false.
Anyway, I should conclude for tonight. Morning games at six. Another reason to hate being here. Why would anyone want to do anything outdoors at six in the morning, in the cold, and the rain? Give me strength and tawakkul.
Yours, Ina

CHAPTER 4

NIDRA

Okay, I take it all back. I don't care for the annual fest even a little bit. And yes, *now* I'm complaining. It's insanely chaotic and stressful, and I don't know how the other captains manage everything, but I always end up running around trying to fix things that have gone wrong at the last minute and I absolutely hate it.

Like this time—I left two tiny things for the costume and props team to figure on their own, just the flower basket for Eliza and the beard for Alfred, and they fucked it up. The flower basket was, well, let's just say no one would buy flowers that look as awful as Eliza before the makeover no matter her bubbly personality, and the beard was more for a fancy salon-going Santa than the poor worker-type person Alfred Doolittle is supposed to be.

And this is on the day of the performance! Which meant that all other houses had used up the props from the art supply and I had to make do with whatever I could find and come up with some sort of beggar beard and half-decent artificial flowers because god forbid the nuns let us pluck some real ones from the school garden.

Fuck ... okay ... there has got to be something here I can work with. Some sort of ink I could use to colour the beard with, and quickly, because otherwise Ignaz is going to have to wear a wet beard and she's not going to love me much when her face is all black and brown and she has to meet her boyfriend like that on the next town outing.

'Oh hey, Inayat.'
She was bent over a pottery wheel in concentration.
'What are you up to?'
'Hey. Pottery?' she replied with a polite smile.
I laughed.

In the last week, I had spoken to Inayat a few times while we worked on the sets for the play, but she barely chatted. Even when she hung out with us that one night when we made the tuck raid, she mostly only said something when asked, except the one suggestion of taking some of the dalle paste to add to the Wai Wai, which I have to admit was kinda genius.

'I can see that, but what are you making?'
'Oh, sorry, just pulling a cylinder.'
'Which you will make into?'
'I don't know.'
'I have lots of days when I run out of ideas too. It's like I have zero creativity!'

She looked up and smiled.

'Why don't you try the electric wheel? The girls say it is much easier.'
'It doesn't make organic rings in the clay like the manual one does,' she said matter-of-factly.

I don't know much about pottery, only the little I've seen girls do during art classes, but Inayat on the wheel was something else. For starters, she seemed to know exactly what she was doing. She looked super profesh cutting off the top of the cylinder and using a thin cloth to curve the edges, sliding the cylinder off the wheel and banging down another lump of clay onto it. And she looked kinda cute doing it all ... confident, which was not how she usually was, and super calm too. Imagine a tiny person banging a big lump of clay with insane force and then kicking the wheel crazy hard before working on the piece with intense focus. It was quite funny and pretty cool at the same time.

I'd never really paid much actual attention to her before, but something about Inayat on the wheel made me stare at her, admiring her big eyes moving with the clay behind her glasses, the ring on her tiny nose that I haven't seen anyone else in school wear twitching a little as she bit her lips in concentration. I hadn't noticed how pretty Inayat actually was, how her cheeks were always slightly pink compared to her pale skin. But, looking at her then, she looked, well ... ugh, I don't even know, I can only think of super corny movie dialogues and that is way too weird for me to say out loud. Plus, I don't remember ever thinking of any girl like that other than Shailene Woodley in the *Divergent Series*. And can you blame me for that one? She was kinda totally amazing in it.

'You look like you've been doing this for years,' I said, shaking the thought off.

'A few now.'

'Do you mind if I sit here with you and do my work?'

'Of course not,' Inayat smiled shortly.

I laid out some newspapers and started work, mixing ink paints with water, dipping the beard into it in bits and then combing it out to remove the excess. I probably looked ridiculous—dipping, holding the beard up against me and combing it down—because I heard Inayat speak on her own.

'What *exactly* are you doing?'

I looked up at her, surprised, the beard still held against my neck. 'Oh, umm ... I'm trying to make it look like it belongs on a drunk garbage man's face?'

Inayat laughed. Actually laughed! And I felt a strange queasy knot in my gut. Weird. Very weird.

'Want to try burning it?' she asked.

'What?'

'Singeing it will curl the hair on the edges and make it look black and prickly in an unwashed way. And it will make the inking you are doing look more real.'

I looked at her, surprised again, as she went back to slide yet another cylinder off the wheel and add it to the line of eight in front of her, each exactly the same as the other, not even kidding.

'Want to help me?'

'Sure.'

She climbed off the pottery wheel and went to the cupboard to look for ... something ... ah, a candle. 'Wow, you clearly know the room a lot more than I have in five years.'

She smiled and lit the candle. 'Will you hold it up and tilt it a little?'

I did and she moved fast—lighting the beard and quickly putting out the flame with a piece of canvas. The beard was ready to be worn by a drunk garbage man in minutes.

'This is perfect! Thank you so much. Can I ask you for one more favour? I have to make these flowers for Eliza's basket.'

'Sure, yes. She sold parma violets, didn't she?'

I looked at her, confused. 'Did she?'

'In the film, *My Fair Lady*. Audrey Hepburn tries to sell parma violets to the Captain. Nana told me they were parma violets.'

'Oh, I dunno,' I responded, looking at her, super impressed. 'So, how do we make these violets you're talking about?'

She went through the supply drawers calmly and pulled out sheets of coloured paper in shades of purple and green, glue, wires and sticky coloured tape. And without a word began cutting them into small shapes and layering them. I saw very little because she moved so fast—putting the wire through them and taping them all together.

'This should do? We can add more leaves once we have a few bunched together,' she said, handing me the flower stick.

'This is ridiculously cute!' I exclaimed. And it really was. 'Show me how to do it.'

We got to work, Inayat guiding me super patiently through the first one, and then we were both making a flower a minute.

'So, how are you liking school now?' I asked between folding and taping.

'It's okay.'

'What do you do in your free time? I know you are helping with the sets with Pema, but now that that is almost done.'

'Pottery. Or I read,' she said, monosyllabic once again.

'Oh! I really hate reading. I love watching movies though, that's why we chose *Pygmalion* for the play—I loved *My Fair Lady*! I used to watch it with my mother all the time.'

'It is a great play.'

'You've read it? It's part of the syllabus in the eleventh grade actually, so you'll read it anyways.'

'I have. I really like Bernard Shaw.'

I stared at her, the knot in my stomach growing. I swear, so fucking weird. What even was this feeling? It was strangely familiar but also completely new—a mix of excitement and ... and something else, I wasn't sure what.

'Have you explored the school beyond the art room and the graveyard?' I asked instead.

'No.'

'How about tonight?' I heard myself say without thought. 'After we've wrapped up the play, let's take a walk. I'll show you around the campus. It's such an old school, even I keep finding hidden places all the time.'

'Sure, that would be nice,' she nodded.

I was surprised she didn't disagree. 'It's a plan then! Of course, unless we lose the play round. Then I'll be sitting sulking in bed with Wai Wai and hot choc.'

'It's a good production you've put together,' she smiled. By now we had finished plenty of sticks and Inayat was putting them together into small bunches.

'No one says that to me and I feel like I need to hear it all the time!' I leaned in to hug her in thanks but managed to tip over the ink bottle instead. 'Oh no!'

'Don't worry,' she smiled, 'I'll take care of this, you go.'

'Thank you so much. This is enough flowers, right?'

'I think so, yes.'

'Good! I'll get going then. We don't have long.'

'Do you need any other help?'

'No, this was great. Thank you. And it was fun. I'll see you at the play. Fingers crossed!'

'See you there. Good luck.'

'Thank you! And to you, we get five points for set design too!'

CHAPTER 5

INAYAT

Dear God,

    Ammi wrote to me again—her second letter in a fortnight. I don't know why she is writing to me; it breaks my heart all over again when she does. I don't want to read two lines of concern-filled 'how are yous' and two pages about her new life in Lucknow and how great things have been with Amir. I don't want to see photos of the house she is busy decorating and the room she says I will stay in when I come 'home'. How can she even think I would want to live with Amir and her after everything she has done? I want to go back to Hyderabad, to Nani Nana and Sidra Di. That is my home. They are. And her writing to me with all this only reminds me of every choice she has made for me that I hate, every bit of grief that she has selfishly brought to our lives, and it only makes me resent her so much more. I wish she would understand this and leave me alone. I know she has called Miss Farzana asking to talk to me, because the matron's come looking a few times, cussing under her breath about parents who refuse to adhere to rules, but I have managed to hide in the bathroom to escape that. I'm sure Nani and Nana have told her about my letters to them, and the phone calls I've made each weekend in the seven minutes of booth time we get.

    I know you wouldn't approve of what I am doing. I know Nani doesn't approve at all either. I'm supposed to love and respect my parents, and I do, but I'm not sure I can do that all the time. And isn't it better that I stay away from Ammi than be dishonest and hurtful about how I truly feel about her right now?

I just don't want to think of her for some time. I'm barely able to make it through the day without breaking down, and thinking about her always makes me want to bawl. It all angers me so much. Not in an aggressive way, no, but I don't remember feeling so much pain ever, not even when Ammi found out about Abba's affair, beat him up and threw him out of the house. That night is still so fresh in my mind—Abba standing outside, begging for forgiveness, begging her to let him in so he could explain. I remember he was freezing in the Delhi winters and I secretly slipped him a sweater, only for Ammi to beat me up for the first time when she found out. She threw me against the wall that day and then a mirror in all her anger. Nani says she didn't mean to hit me, that she was never angry at me but hurt by everything and only had me. I was angry at Ammi Abba both, and I didn't want to leave Abba or Delhi, but at least I understood why she decided to move to Hyderabad. And I didn't feel betrayed then. I do now.

Of course, pottery helps, and I am so blessed that they have a good art studio here. I pulled fourteen cylinders today, and it felt very calming to just sit at the wheel, not thinking about anything except working with the clay. I was telling Nana about it the other day and he asked me why I wasn't making the sculptures I was back in Hyderabad. I wish I could tell him how I feel like my mind is incapable of coming up with anything creative without drowning in all the other thoughts that come pouring in. I suppose cylinders will have to do for now. They are mundane and seem like just what I need to block out the noise in my head. Maybe I can take all of them and create an installation, title it 'Healing from Childhood'.

Although, honestly, it was so much fun crafting those beards and flowers with Nidra. She's like sunshine, Nidra is, in a way that Nani always talks about those who are your children, and being around her is always very light, joyful even. I look forward to seeing her around the school these days, in fact I look out for her. It's as if something in *me wants to spend all the time I can with her. I know I almost jumped at her offer to show me around after the play.*

I am sure she was tired from all the running around, and her friends were calling her to celebrate our win, but she insisted that we go for the walk we had decided on.

We sneaked up to the attic of the administrative block and through to the nuns' quarters—one of whom had just baked a fruit cake in the common kitchen that we ate a slice of, scrumptious might I just add (please don't punish me; I promise I'll read an extra hundred count of astaghfar after namaz tonight. It just felt so nice to go along with her). And we took a quick tour of one of their rooms, which was like nothing I had ever seen or even imagined. I mean, the whole school seems old, and it is, but this felt ancient—like time had stood still here and the flickering candle was the only sign of life, although even that felt like a computer simulation now that I think about it. The room was the smallest I'd ever seen, with white panelled walls and old wood floors—furnished with a simple bed, a window with lace curtains, a small praying corner and a writing desk. It felt little, but also ... peacefully enough. You know what I mean? It reminded me of what Nani always tells me—that I must be content with living an honest and hardworking life and leave the rest to you.

But before I had time to soak in what it made me feel, we had to rush back because we heard some of the nuns coming up. And on our way back we bumped into Nidra's friends, who insisted we come back to the common room where the celebrations were still going on.

I really didn't want to keep her from it again, even though it was the last place I wanted to be, so I went with her, hoping I could sneak out soon enough.

And I did. Nidra introduced me to all her friends—so many I lost count—and I spent some time sitting in on the games and celebrations, but thankfully slipped out the first chance I got, because while they were fun, and very nice to me, they seemed to love to gossip a little too much and I didn't enjoy that at all. And I definitely didn't like how judgemental they all seemed about so many things. I mean, I couldn't even imagine the things they said about Priya's body in that costume *for the play, let alone say it out loud in front of so many people; and what they thought of Ruchika's family made me wonder what they would make of mine if they knew.*

So, here I am, writing to you.

It's strange. Nidra is nothing like me. I mean, the first thing you think about when you see her is how beautiful she is. Every time I see her, I seem to find something new that makes me think so. But, more importantly, she is so friendly and outgoing ... jovial ... popular even. She seems like she can talk to anyone, make everyone laugh and have fun. And yet, in the little time we've spent together, it's just calming to be around her, and I feel ... strange comfort. It's as if all the knots in my stomach disappear when I'm with her. There is no judgement, no questions or unnecessary counsel, and I can just be, which is new, and rather nice. I have never had that with anyone before, that lightness of feeling free of emotional baggage, like we get to leave it on the side for a little bit and not be reminded of it. It feels very special, what we are starting to share.

Thank you for bringing me to her. Nani says I complain to you a lot and am not grateful enough. I promise I am trying to do better; I promise I will try to be better.

Until next time. I love you.

Yours, Ina

CHAPTER 6

PEMA

You know those like seriously brave times when instead of predicting what your parents are going to say you actually ask them for what you want? They've probably said no like a gazillion times before, so you think they'll do it again. I mean, what the hell, they always say no. But you have like this new motivation, this fire or something that is making you do it. What's the harm anyways, right? So prepared for a no but manifesting a yes, you ask.

That is exactly what I did. Inayat's totally begun to feel like a real friend—the kind I have always wanted but never had. I guess it has helped that she's super quiet, so she hasn't found other friends, but I don't even think it is like that with her. Not like the many other new girls who have come over the years and completely forgotten me after a few weeks except when they needed favours. No, Inayat's not like any of them. Plus, like, I don't think she can actually be mean to anyone. We've spent a lot of time together in the last few weeks in class and out working on the sets, and I just couldn't imagine not being in school with her on the final days of the performances. So I asked my parents if I could stay the final fest nights in school.

And you know how once you've asked, done your job, and you're feeling like relieved but also anxious as hell all at the same time while you wait for their reply, and they actually surprise you with the answer you want but aren't expecting? You know? Mine did! They said yes! I was standing in Inayat's dorm, putting away my clothes in her bedside table, and I still couldn't believe it. I was going to stay in school, for three whole nights!

No 3:30 p.m. bell to tell me I have to go home for three full days, thank you very much. I could spend all day with my best friend (ya, I am pretty sure that she is mine), and nights too! Of course, we don't know if Inayat thinks I'm her best friend and all. I hope she does, I mean ... I *think* she does. But we can't be completely sure I guess.

Although the first evening I was pretty sure we were.

We were done working on the sets and didn't really have anything to do until the performances the next day, so, like most other girls, decided to spend Friday evening just like roaming around the school and making the most of the rules not being totally anal that weekend. That and Wai Wai night!

Fuck, I mean, I don't even know if I can like fully describe what it was like taking our Wai Wai bowls and Bournvita to the hill by the mess and watching the lights come on in the houses across the hills that night along with Charu, Shivangi and some of the other girls from class.

Aama, Baba and I go for late-night walks in town all the time (Aama says it's her favourite time of the day, when everything is more like silent or whatever, and so Baba makes sure we do it at least once a week. The two of them are very cute and in love like that). And every time we cross the Governor's bungalow, we buy bowls of piro aloo and butter teas from the shack right opposite and sit down and eat until the aloo makes our noses drip—in Aama's case hiccup like crazy—sipping the sweet tea in between. I love looking at the lights shine across the town in so many colours, pointing out the houses I will buy for Aama Baba once I become rich, how I have no idea yet. When I was in a local school, Tenzing and Dawa would sleep over at my place and we would all go together sometimes. Those were the best times of my life, until they found a new group once I left.

But sitting with Inayat was totally a dream come true.

'The town looks stunning, no?' I commented.

'It really does,' she said.

'Do you miss home?'

I've known Inayat for like some weeks now, and here are the things I have learned about her. She loves pottery and is great at making cylinders (she had twenty-seven when I last counted and Sir Lama was going to let her fire them at the end of term). She reads a lot, and I mean really lots. She loves shahi toast, because she always eats her own and mine (I get her gulab jamun when we get those). She also has a thing for mushroom matar. And she really doesn't like talking about her family. I've tried to ask her about like her home and family so many times, but she always changes the topic.

'It's nothing like this,' she replied.

See what I mean by avoiding the topic? 'But what's it like?' I prodded.

'I don't know ...' she said, and she went into a bit of a 'mulling mood' (as Aama calls them), looking so sad that I gave up and changed topics myself.

'I'm going to be so hated in Darj if I say this, and I might have to move like really far away, but I like Maggi more than Wai Wai, even the new Indomie thing that's come over Wai Wai. I'm actually loving Mama Noodles the most of late. Of course I'm talking cooked stuff. I guess raw you can only really pick Wai Wai. Although I know some of the girls in school got really sick some months ago and we found out it was because they had been eating one of those raw noodles,' I said. And because she only gave a short laugh, I continued, 'Which one would you pick?'

'That's tough. I think I'd say Wai Wai, but the one made in Nepal now that I know the difference.' She gave another one of her small smiles, the ones she kind of gives more because I changed the topic and not because of the conversation itself.

'No way! Hey, Charu, Wai Wai or Maggi?'

'Duh! Wai Wai!' Charu screamed.

'What about you, Shivangi?'

'Mama I think, but between Maggi and Wai Wai, has to be Wai Wai.'

And the chain continued, ending with all the girls on the hill choosing Wai Wai.

'Okay then! Now you've really got to promise to like take my secret to the grave or whatever,' I whispered to Inayat.

Inayat laughed. 'Okay.'

I can literally count the number of times Inayat has laughed this loud since we've been friends. Thrice, including this one. The first time was when this stupid ass pigeon followed me around the whole fruit break trying to get my apple, and when I hit it with a book, it flew over and shat on my head instead. The second was like a smaller one, like this time, when Miss Gardner decided to play my latest music composition in front of the entire class as like an example of what is the best worst music of all times. I mean, really, what do they want when we are forced to do music classes. Not like I'd have any other great hobby or whatever, but still. And the third was today.

I actually really like it when Inayat laughs. She has like these huge eyes, and even more ginormous lashes—unlike me. I have the tiniest eyes and am almost bald when it comes to eyelashes, although Aama always scolds me when I say I'm ugly, with an even uglier flat nose, and tells me that I'm beautiful, with nice Tibetan features and great milky skin and long silky hair. But I guess she has to say that because she is my mother. I might believe it if a boy said it to me, but obviously no one has till now. Anyways, that's not Inayat. Inayat is like actually pretty. Maybe not like Nidra, who could pass of as a Bollywood actress, but whenever Inayat smiles you can see her eyes like sparkle like crazy, and then she has these tiny freckles on her cheeks that look so cute and happy, like that Strawberry Shortcake cartoon. You want to instantly pull her cheeks.

'I just cannot believe you didn't say Maggi,' I continued, actually disappointed.

And that is how the rest of the evening went, debating Maggi vs. Wai Wai, and me going on and on about all my Wai Wai memories—over cold picnics and warm evenings around the gao bonfire and on the house terrace with Errol barking around us for a bite. (In case you haven't guessed, Errol is our dog, a Tibetan Shih Tzu gifted to me by Dada for my thirteenth birthday and named after the Weasley owl, because he was as weird and annoyingly silly as Errol when he was a puppy. He still is actually. Of course, not to say I don't love him and all. I do! So much. But, anyways, super random info to give right now.)

The second evening zoomed by. The performances went on forever and ever, and by the end of it we were all tired as hell and just wanted to get to bed.

Oh, wait, I haven't talked about the dorms at St Mary's, no? Well, they're pretty basic really. Every room has three parts of sorts—the bathroom, the dressing area that has like all the lockers and dressing mirrors and stuff, and the dorm itself. The junior school, from grades five to eight, have bunk beds and there are twelve girls in a room with four bathrooms and four bathing areas. For the ninth grade to the twelfth, you have four to six girls in a room and two bathrooms and bathing areas. Apparently it's the school's way of teaching the girls how to adjust and manage time well or something. I guess I should put this on my list of things to be grateful for in my current life.

Inayat's dorm has six beds, but there are only five girls in it right now—the sixth recently left school because she kept getting unwell all the time. It happens a lot here. The Darjeeling climate isn't super easy to get used to. It like crazy cold for most of the year, and it's raining for the rest. I'm not saying there aren't like sunny days, but there's this like mildew, musty kind of moist thing that is always there and that takes a lot of getting used to. There is also the whole thing of settling in a boarding school away from home. I mean, I can crib about my like current school situation and all, but I can't imagine being away from Aama Baba for too long. I have decided, when I leave for college or work, I'll still be close by, like Dada is, and keep coming home every chance I get. Although I think Dada comes home too much. I love him and all, but every time he comes, I have to empty his room and go back to my small one, and that is so annoying. But like, I can't *actually* complain about that. We have so much fun, the four of us. We're always doing fun things together. Plus, when Dada is here Aama cooks all her best stuff. I guess it's a love-hate relationship, which could possibly be the story of my life now that I think about it.

Anyways, what was I saying … ya, the Darjeeling mould. Also, I haven't heard of anyone leaving because of it, but St Mary's is weirdly filled with lice. Not even the normal amount at all. Like only a few months ago one of the juniors got infested so bad that they were falling off on her bed and all over her clothes. They had to shave her hair off and burn her clothes to get rid of them. And no, I am not kidding! Poor thing, she is bald and all the girls make fun of her. Now *that* is definitely something to leave school for I would think.

Anyways, again! Back to the empty bed, because it was only thanks to it that I got to sleep over. St Mary's has a super weird strict policy when it comes to this. We've heard of the principal going completely mental when girls have been like 'caught' sharing a bed, because god forbid they were 'sinning' and being 'un-ladylike' and 'lesbians' or whatever the hell they think chilling in the same bed means, and it's always ended like really badly. But with the empty bed Inayat and I could have like a real sleepover, and that was super exciting, even if it meant just going to bed completely dead and not having like the 2 a.m. heart-to-hearts that I have heard a lot of the girls talk about.

Well, it *was* very exciting, for the first two days anyways, until the horrible third evening. It made me doubt our whole friendship and think it's all in my head like so many other things, forget like me being her actual best friend.

The fest had just gotten over and our house, even though like insanely close to a win, lost to second position. Not a bad place to be. I mean, considering we had come third for years now, but Nidra did not take it super well. I mean, she didn't throw a fit or anything, but I could see she was upset as hell. So her friends decided to still have the party they had planned for when they won and called Inayat for it.

'Hey, Inayat. We'll see you in the common room for the party?' Riya yelled as we walked back from the concert hall to the residential blocks. Oh ya, the school has the fanciest, most ginormous concert hall right behind the church where we put up two performances every year—one for the fest and the other for the town. To be fair, I quite like this bit about the school.

'Ya ya, come. I'm sure Nidra would like it,' continued Ignaz.

I looked at Inayat, super surprised. *Nidra would like it? What the hell did that mean?* I didn't even think Nidra really knew Inayat, forget like actually wanting her at her party.

'Umm ... I don't know,' Inayat replied.

'Oh, come on babe. We have a whole game of Pictionary planned and we need you on our team,' Riya swore.

'You wish she is on your team,' Ignaz teased.

'Shut up you guys. We'll flip for it,' said Nitisha. 'Now come, Inayat! And Pema, why don't you come too?'

I looked at Nitisha, completely shook. *Inayat played Pictionary with Nidra and her friends? The Inayat I knew hardly even spoke to people around her, and this one played board games with the seniors? When did this happen? How? And why didn't Inayat tell me anything about it?* The mini-me was yelling in my head.

But I didn't have much time to think then, because we were dragged to the common room, which was totally ready for a party and already pretty loud with the celebrations.

For the rest of the evening, I just hung out with Inayat like she was a stranger or something. She wasn't super chatty with the other girls, only a little with Nidra (although I did notice her smile and even laugh when they talked—*so she does this with someone else too*, of course my mind piped up), but she was like focused while we played Pictionary, Taboo and Scattergories. And Riya was right, she really was good at Pictionary. *Another thing you didn't know about her.*

Could this really be the same Inayat I had known and thought was my best friend? Wouldn't best friends share things about themselves? At least important stuff like being friends with the house captain and hanging out with her and her friends if not the like the deepest, darkest secrets?

I was totally zoned out all night. I couldn't think of anything else, not even when Miss Farzana came to chase all of us back to the dorms. I zombied my way up and obviously didn't think of anything else once I was in bed. Ugh, I even dreamed about it—of Inayat hanging out with Nidra and her friends while I stood in a corner looking at all of them. And they walked through me like I was invisible, and I kept yelling at them to make them notice me, but it was like they just couldn't hear me. I woke up in quite a dump, but when Inayat asked if I was ready for breakfast, I decided to just shut my mind as much as I could. *Like you can afford to be all mopey with her right now anyways*, my mind added.

CHAPTER 7

INAYAT

Dear God,
    For the first time in a long time, I am not writing to you with complaints. Not because I have found the liberation of having none; I am still angry and it will take a while to let it all go, but I spoke with Nani today and she got very upset when I told her that I was mad at you for taking me away from her. She told me that I must not be distrustful of your plan for me—and because I cannot let go of the anger without being dishonest with her, and because I am sure you would know even if I tried to pretend otherwise, I have decided to resign myself to how things are as of now. Plus, I did promise you I would try to complain less. I suppose I can find solace in the fact that it was the same when we moved to Hyderabad too. I only learned to have tawakkul and saw your will over time. I want to believe the same now. It is the only way really. As kids we don't get to decide for ourselves, do we?
    And, I suppose things haven't been all that bad.
    Classes are just fine. I prefer to keep my head low and do what is required, but that seems to be working, and I'm grateful for it. And it's nice having Pema around. I know I don't talk to her much, sometimes I feel afraid to talk about my life. Plus, she has so much to say all the time, and I like listening to her chattering away. It is comforting to hear of her life with her mum and dad, to know of happy families,

and I think she likes it when I hear her complain about the goings-on at home. Like today, when she was complaining about her mother making her clean after Errol, who had contracted a stomach infection after eating something strange in the forest. I feel that Pema has a great ability to love, and the need to give it uninhibitedly, much like me, something I feel she has learned from her mother, as I have from Nani. Did I tell you her mother now regularly sends me some of her homemade chebureki because I liked the Tibetan snack so much the first time? Every time I tell Nani of Pema, she tells me I must thank you for the blessing of a great friend, and I truly am beginning to feel like Pema is one.

I've never had many friends as you know. There was Arshia in Delhi, but we lost touch after I moved to Hyderabad, and that was tough. But then I had Nani Nana, Sidra Di and Manisha Ma'am, and it felt like enough. Anyway, it was easier that way, the girls in Hyderabad were a little too nosy about Ammi and Abba's divorce. But yes, Pema feels like an honest friend. Although I often find it hard when she asks me questions about home and my family. I wish she wouldn't. But at least she has gotten used to my silences and doesn't prod me for answers anymore.

Nidra is the opposite. She never asks questions, although I feel like if she asked, I might not hesitate to tell her. There's an unfamiliar sense of ease I feel with Nidra that I am getting used to, like I could share everything about me with her. Not that Pema has ever made me feel otherwise, not at all; it's just that with Pema listening to her and sharing laughs with her gives me joy, and I want to live in that bubble. With Nidra, there is this oneness, like she'll understand without me having to explain a word, no judgement. But it's like all that matters to her is the present moment, and it is so peaceful to just be around her, sitting together in the graveyard, journaling, reading, listening to music. The time I spend with her friends is okay too. I still dislike how much they gossip, but I have come to not altogether mind the evenings with them. Ignaz, Riya, Nitisha are all nice to me, and we always end up doing something I wouldn't usually do, which makes for great letters to Nani and Nana, who are peeved when I tell them I spent my days reading or in the art room. I do prefer being with Nidra, just us, though. There is something about her that fills me with hope like nothing I have felt before. Even though I sometimes wish we didn't always have to be in the graveyard when we are alone. But Nidra says the girls can make up nasty rumours about two girls hanging alone all the time, especially not from the same grade, and honestly it feels like she is so bothered by the thought that I don't insist otherwise. Graveyard or not, our time together has quickly become what I look forward to. In fact, now that I think about it, a big part of me only spends time with her friends so I can be around her more, something I haven't cared for before.

I guess I am also lucky that the school library and art studio are open until lights out, because even though I now spend most of my nights with Nidra after everyone's slept off, I don't know what I would have done in the evenings, once Pema's left, and on nights when Nidra is busy with other things, had it not been for my hours on the pottery wheel and reading in the library. You will also be happy to know that I started my first hand-built Tina Vlassopulos-inspired pot. I even spoke to Sir Lama about letting me draw on the cylinders and put together a Founder's Day installation. Nana will be so happy to see them when he comes for it.

But well, that's that. I don't have more to tell you and I have to go meet Nidra in the graveyard now.

Yours, Ina

CHAPTER 8

PEMA

Every weekend, St Mary's has this town outing thing where girls get to go out into town for like half a day (I know it sounds like cattle being let out for like grazing or something, but it's much better than that, so the girls say). It used to be twice a month for each class, but because of some political unrest type situation in town it has been cut to one. Anyways, I don't know much about what's happening. I mean, like, you might be fifteen but your parents still want to pretend you're like a fucking child when it comes to serious things, right? Although, of course this logic doesn't exist with like work around the house and how hard you need to be studying for the future that's coming tomorrow and stuff. But honestly, it's not like I really care to find out myself either. There are just more important things happening in my life right now.

It was Inayat's first weekend outing and she seemed kind of nervous about it. And it made sense why. She'd be all alone in a new town. She wasn't really friendly with the girls in our class. *And luckily for you the school outings happen in class batches and the tenth grade goes with the ninth and not the eleventh*, my super evil mind said. So, I promised to meet her below the school and take her around town. She only had to come down one hill, and I asked Shefali to help if she asked.

I badly wanted to show her some of my favourite spots, so I like planned it properly. A quick trip to the market so she could pick up the things she needed, a stop for a super big and super yummy lunch of Nepali and Tibetan food at my favourite restaurant—if you can call like the hole-in-the-wall Nawang's that—where you could order everything on the menu and still not have to pay more than 300, and last a hot chocolate at Keventers. We wouldn't be able to do more than that.

So, I got there before time, looking for her in all the St Mary's girls coming down the hill.

'Hey, Shef. Have you seen Inayat?' I asked as I saw Shefali come down.

'She was right behind, babe. She should be down soon. Want us to wait with you?'

'No no, it's okay. Thanks.'

'Pems!' Charu squealed. What you doing here? Anyways, you've got to come with us. We're going to meet Ragini's St Stephen's boyfriend and he said he's coming with his friends if you know what I mean! Do you like my blush princess look?'

Considering the only time I had gone out with girls from my class was when the school organized like a one-day class 'trip' to a squash making factory in Jorethang followed by a picnic by the river, forget being actually invited to hang out with them and their boyfriends, I would have jumped at the chance, but today was not going to be the day.

'Oh fun! And ya, love what's going on with that like burnt pink blush situation. Totally winning! But I'm waiting for Inayat actually, have to show her around and stuff, but tell me all about meeting our handsome Hasan,' I giggled.

'Sshhhhh,' Charu giggled. 'And yes!'

'Oh, there she is—Ina!' I shouted, spotting her coming down. 'I'll see you in school, Charu, have fun!'

'See you! Good luck to me!' Charu rushed down to the others.

Inayat looked up from her book and waved back.

How does someone read a book while walking ... down a hill?

I guess, I suppose, books can help people feel less alone or something. I mean, I know I feel lonely as hell all the time and reading actually helps me forget things, for some time anyways. But I don't think anyone can read as much as Inayat does. It feels like she's read everything already. I swear, every time I've told her what I'm reading, she's gone on about how she liked the book, or didn't like it, before giving me really annoying details about the author and writing and whatnot. Like that day when I picked up the Wodehouse book she recommended and she said something about how Wodehouse said he ignored real life in his writing and wrote musical comedy without music or something. I have no idea what she meant because I hardly ever pay attention beyond the stories and characters. But it's the only time she talks a little without me forcing her like a total psycho, so I listen to her anyways.

'Okay, I've planned our whole day.'

We took a walk around Mall Road, down the zoo road, around St Stephen's (the boys are way better looking than the geeky ones from St George's by the way. Also, I mean, what's with the ugly black umbrella they carry everywhere) to the Happy Valley Tea Estate and then back into the main town market. I've mentioned it's my favourite way around the town, no? Second favourite actually. I like taking the longer Lover's Road with Aama Baba, because it literally has the best view of the Kanchenjunga range compared to anywhere in town—the mountains feel like crazy close, as if you could roll down the hill and land right on their feet or something. But we aren't allowed there in school uniform (after some kids got caught making out there and smoking up and stuff) and I couldn't really like take the risk in broad daylight, could I!?

'Okay, let's pick up everything you need from here,' I said, pointing at the shambled mess of a shopping centre that Mahakal Market is.

'I only need a birthday card and a diary, mine is over,' Inayat replied.

'Whose birthday is it?' I asked, pretty sure she wouldn't tell me anyways, like all other times I asked her anything personal.

'Nani's.'

'Oh,' I said, surprised that she gave me an answer. 'There's an Archies right here,' I continued, pointing at the card shop down a narrow lane. 'I also need to buy a few things for home.'

Inayat suggested that I finish the tasks on Aama's list and she hers so we could get to lunch on time. And, I mean, it would have been fun to do it all together, but it made more sense to get to Nawang's before it got like really crowded. So we split up—me getting the meat weighed and cleaned, the cloth for the puja room measured and cut, getting Dawa Daju to put new movies on my pen drive—and met again at the gates.

'Let's go this way. It will be much shorter,' I told her, pushing her through the crowded lanes and towards some narrow moss-covered stairs.

'Pema, what are these flags?' Inayat asked as we marched up saathi seedi (literally meaning sixty stairs).

I still get shocked sometimes when Inayat actually asks me stuff on her own, which I guess is pretty stupid because she's started talking a whole lot more now than when she first came; and I've noticed she can get quite like chatty about some stuff, really chatty in fact. Like the other day when she got really caught up talking about some children's book about Roald Dahl's time in boarding school and how that helped him think up Willy Wonka, and his time in the RAF during World War II that inspired the gremlins or whatever. And I've also noticed she gets weirdly excited about ghost stories, but that's just a super random fact. Anyways, moving on.

'These,' she whispered, pointing at the green, yellow and white flags with 'Gorkhaland' written on them that were everywhere.

I shushed her. 'I'll tell you when we sit down for lunch.'

She nodded. (I sometimes like how she is never annoying about asking questions, even though I know I can be, and even though sometimes it would be nice if she would actually be annoying and want to keep talking too.)

And so we quietly walked up and through the town to Nawang's.

I would describe the walk and everything, I obviously love giving details, but, honestly, there isn't anything that I could tell that will not make anyone hate the town and not want to come here, just because it's the crowded, mucky part of everyday markets, so probably better to avoid that.

At Nawang's, I ordered all my family favourites. Ema datshi, tingmo, sha phaley, piro aloo with all the achaar and chutneys and stuff (you can't *not* have those, Dada calls it 'the whole shebang'), some sweet butter tea—and a bowl of fried Wai Wai (eye roll and moving on!) because, if Dada is to be believed, if you don't have the fried Wai Wai at Nawang's, you might as well go bury yourself alive or whatever.

We made it in good time too, because while we waited for our food, the place quickly filled up with people taking bowls of thukpa from the counter and crowding around the TV to watch some angry political debate.

'He's wearing the same flag we saw around town today ...' Inayat whispered.

'Oh, ya, okay I'll tell you now. That's the head of the ruling party in the hills. Baba thinks that there might be an agitation in the town or something. So, like recently, the state education minister I think brought out some three-language policy type thing and made Bengali compulsory. And obviously the town people got pissed as hell because there aren't that many Bengalis in Darjeeling anyways, and making the language compulsory was like so dumb. I mean imagine us having to learn Bengali too! I would have died. But anyways, Baba says it's becoming a bigger political issue and the whole like old movement to create a new state could be starting again. Plus, apparently, they lost really badly in some elections in Mirik and they're not happy about the masses being brainwashed into the change.'

'What does that mean?'

'I don't know really. Baba says that the movement got completely nuts in the 1980s. The town was shut down and there was like crazy violence and stuff. Some thousands of people died and the town was completely destroyed in the fight between the local and state parties. They basically are demanding a separate state because they feel like we aren't treated like equals and aren't receiving the financial benefits because we are a small vote bank. Plus they feel like we are very different, culturally and stuff, and treated like minorities. A separate state would bring more independence to the governance here, Baba says, which will help us all. So ya, Baba thinks that if it is anything like then, and apparently with the current leader it may be, it could be like full blown.'

'And what will *that* mean?'

Wow, could I have asked for anything when I wished that Ina would annoy me with questions just a few moments ago? my mind laughed.

'Who the fuck knows man. I have only overheard all this in bits, on the news and when Aama Baba are whispering in their room. They like refuse to tell me anything themselves, and, honestly, I don't care, it's not like it is affecting us right now anyways.'

'How can you say for certain it won't later, Pema! You have to find out. Will there be an actual conclusion to it? Are you sure it will help locals?' Inayat whispered.

'Baba says it is actually for our good, that hopefully this time the centre will bring about some action. But I don't know, I've only heard these things.'

'You have to know,' Inayat continued. She really was talking a lot and I liked that. 'If it will affect you, how can you not care?'

But our conversation was interrupted by the incoming food.

'Okay no, food first!' I declared. 'Please, please, please! Nothing's happening right now. And I promise I will try find out more, okay.'

I showed Ina how to dip the tingmo into the ema datshi and how the sweet sel roti tasted best with the piro aloo, and we slurped momo dunked in like literally the most insanely amazeballs ajinomoto-loaded soup, and we forgot about the television and the agitation.

Only for a little bit though. Because, as I should have known, when I met Ina the next day in school, she was sitting with a heap of newspapers on the desk and the fattest book I had ever seen on her lap, ready (I can't really figure why) to hit me with concerns and questions as soon as I walked in.

'You have to read this, Pem. I didn't say much yesterday because I didn't know enough about what was happening. But I've been reading all night and I don't think you could even think the agitation would be the right thing to happen with the current leaders if you knew,' she said.

'Knew what, Ina?' I just couldn't understand why Ina had turned political activist.

'What happened in the 1980s. So many innocent lives were lost. And only for it to all be repeated two decades later with someone new looking for power? And was there really any benefit for the people? If the person then had really brought improvement, how could the townspeople so easily swap him for a new person? Or are we saying the townspeople didn't have much of a mind of their own to take a stand for themselves? Did it really only take the new man supporting a local singer into winning a reality competition for them to switch sides? Is that really devotion to the town and cause for them?'

The girl went on and on. I mean, fuck, I was literally shook.

'See, Ina. Baba says ...'

'No Pema, you have to read for yourself too. I mean, you can say it hasn't been proven, but do we really believe that the brutal killing of a political leader in 2010 was not assisted by this so-called new leader if not actually planned and executed by him? And what has he even done in all these years? Some unchartered things here and there, but was there really thought behind any of it? You talk about this yourself, right? How bad the water crisis in town has always been, how every year the town suffers from landslides, how the tea trade is suffering, how tourism still isn't great, how bad the construction in town is, the garbage disposal problem. And this is the man you think is okay to support?'

I could see her getting very agitated.

'Ina, you have to wait.' And she finally took a breath. 'I don't know enough either, but I know Baba does, and what he says seems to make sense. You won't understand how it feels to be the other ones.'

'You haven't ever been out of the town; how do you know what being the other one feels like? And don't we all feel like the other in some way? You think I don't feel like the other when there are so many ways my community is shunned?'

I couldn't believe Ina. My shy, soft Ina was saying all this, was misunderstanding me like this. It was all so unlike her.

'Ina, fuck, I mean, okay look around. I am in a boarding school where there is no one like me, no one looks like me or anything, and no one treats me like an actual friend. I think I literally know what being the other means. And if the town feels anything like that, it's just horrible. And I know I would really like if it wasn't like this. So ya, I do get it when Baba says if there is anything that can change that it would be nice. And what do you even really know? From one night of mugging up facts and opinions you think you know what is happening and what should? I mean … honestly. Anyways.'

I can't believe you just said all that. You've totally lost the one friend you had here. You totally lost it on her. For the first time I thought my mind was right, even though I couldn't tell one thought from the other, hurt by everything she said, scared of losing her and angry to defend Baba.

'Pema … I didn't. But I do think …'

But we were cut short by Sir John coming in. And as the day went on, there was just so much to like say that it turned into nothing as we went about the daily stuff.

… and I guess we didn't expect that Baba was going to be right, and things would change so much, so quickly that we would not have time or space to talk about like anything, and I would have to live with the familiar fear that I would once again be totally friendless for what would seem forever.

CHAPTER 9

NIDRA

I hate studying. Absolutely hate. I am pretty decent at it. I score averagely well too, I mean, thank god. But I would give anything to avoid it. Plus, what's the point? I want to be a dancer. How are maths formulas or annoying details of the world's topography really going to help me?

See, languages I get. Even history, because at least I can do something with those stories in my dance, like we did in the house fest. Everyone loved our rendition of Begum Hazrat Mahal's rebellion against the East India Company. If only they had also liked our best of Panic! At The Disco a cappella performance. I guess it was just a little too much. But that's old news. I don't think any of girls (including me now) really regrets it because it was so much fun. Anyways, as I was saying, hate studying!

Which is why I was super pumped when the unit tests were over. No more worrying about studying for at least another five months. And if that didn't call for a party, I dunno what would. Of course, with our luck, the sisters and teachers didn't think so, so we had to come up with a plan of our own.

'Okay, so Riya and I will get the Wai Wai and Bournvita from the mess pantry once Sir Khan has left for the day,' said Ignaz. 'Nidra, you keep watch. That way if there is any change of plans, you can walk out saying you were looking for girls out of bed.'

'Don't forget the Maggi. And try see if you can find some biscuit packets for later, we are very low on stock,' I added, Ignaz giving me a judgy look.

'What! I like Maggi, and I've emptied all my dry tuck, even the little I got in the one town outing during the tests. This whole political unrest is really killing our tuck situation dude. It needs to end soon, whatever this is,' I complained. Although I know I didn't really need to explain, we all got the same measly portion of two packets of biscuits, a small chocolate bar and a juice pouch every week as school-sanctioned tuck that couldn't last more than two days. And with lesser outings because of the political things happening in town we hadn't been able to sneak in enough of our own.

'Fine!' Riya said.

'Who all are coming by the way?' Nitisha piped. 'Apart from the four of us I mean.'

'I told Vrinda and Tanvi to come,' Riya said.

'And I asked Avantika and Roshni,' Ignaz added.

'Oh ... and ... umm ... I bumped into Anjani and invited her,' stammered Nitisha.

'Dude! If that bitch snitches on us, I am going to kill you,' Riya said.

'No no, she won't. She was cornered that time. And Miss Tiwari *had* seen some of us coming out of the computer room,' defended Nitisha.

'You mean she saw *you* come out after sending your mushy email to that idiot Rahul!' Riya laughed. 'I'm telling you, that ick of a boyfriend of yours is going to get us killed someday. Does he even remember it's your birthday next week?'

'Okay, moving on guys,' I interjected. 'And I asked Inayat to come too.'

'Oh yes, she is great with the games!' Nitisha said, happy for the topic change.

'But aren't we going down to the lake?'

'Yes, that's the plan.'

'Doesn't mean we can't play Taboo at the lake, does it?'

We went on for some time longer, sorting the plan out. It is insanely important to know exactly what you are doing when carrying out a sneak party like this. These were the rules—we were gonna divide into groups. Riya, Ignaz and I would handle the food. Nitisha would be in charge of making sure the music and games reached the lake. Vrinda was getting her camping stove and cutlery. Everyone was instructed to wear their swimming costumes under their clothes, and a special note was made for nose and ear buds for the tadpoles in the lake. And, most importantly, we were all to get to the lake at intervals of twenty minutes each, starting with Nitisha at nine, followed by Inayat, Tanvi and Vrinda, Avantika and Roshni and finally the three of us.

And it worked! Getting the food from the mess pantry was cakewalk, as uzhe. Sir Khan never makes a note of his stock, which works in our favour, so Riya and Ignaz managed to get plenty of everything, including my favourite Jim Jam! I have to admit, I slid a few down my jacket for later. By the time we got down to the lake, everyone was in the middle of a game of Taboo, and some of them had already been for a swim.

'Finally!' exclaimed Nitisha, pulling us into the corner behind the hedges.

'Sssshhhh,' Avantika shushed.

'Can we get going on the food already?' Nitisha whispered, realizing her mistake. 'We're starving.'

'Where is the camping stove?'

'It's behind the rose bushes ... wait ... yes ... there.'

'Fuck, it's not here!'

'Ssshhhh.'

'Wait, let me get it ... here it is. Was behind the marigold bushes, sorry. I'll get it going. What are we making first?'

'Can we start with the Wai Wai. This thing takes forever to heat.'

'Hey, at least it will get you hot Wai Wai.'

'No cap, can't complain.'

'Let's play another round of Taboo while we wait.'

'I think I'll go for a swim,' I said.

I really love swimming in the lake. We aren't allowed to, but on one of the nights I was at the graveyard I decided to try my luck, and apart from having to sneeze out a few tadpoles and a harmless ear infection, it was so worth it. And, well, that was that. I told some of the gang and we made a night of it one day, and it has become an after-exam ritual ever since.

'Can I come along?' asked Inayat.

'Of course! Anyone else?'

As suspected, no one cared for a swim once they could smell the Wai Wai. So, Inayat and I went alone.

I can't remember how long we swam. Turns out, Inayat has taken a few diving courses and had an underwater torch and snorkels—that girl always manages to surprise me—and we were in there for a long time. You know how in *Zindagi Na Milegi Dobara* Katrina Kaif and Hrithik Roshan spend what feels like forever together underwater, and you're kinda bored and want to ask the makers to get to the point but also it feels intensely like just them and the ocean? Not gonna lie, it felt like that, but real, with a lot less mindless twirling and a lot more blurry and green. And I can't really figure what it means when I say this and I am completely weirded out by the fact that I am at all, but I think I understood what Hrithik felt when Katrina took his hand and guided him through the water, showing him what life could be or whatever. I am sure I had the same look on my face, even when we got out, all emo and stuff.

But I had no time to make sense of what was going on in my head because we had bowls of lukewarm Wai Wai shoved into our hands as soon as we got out.

'What were you two doing there for so long! We kept calling for you! The Maggi is also almost done, and then we are making hot chocolate,' said Riya.

'Ear plugs!' I said, taking mine out.

'Thank you,' Inayat smiled, taking her bowl.

I looked at Inayat. 'Where did you learn to dive?'

'I don't know it well enough, I can do shallow dives, and deeper ones with an instructor. I went for a few with my dad.'

'So cool! I wish I could do that too. Where have you been for a dive so far?'

'Well, mostly around India. My dad used to say that we never need to go abroad because there is so much to see in India.'

'Used to?'

'I don't see him much anymore. My parents are divorced,' she said, looking away.

It was funny how we had spent so much time together, how close I felt to her, like really nothing I had felt before with any of my friends, and I knew so little about her life outside of school.

'Oh,' I said. I couldn't find the words, but I knew what I actually really wanted to do was to reach out and hold her hand, to comfort her and say I was here for her.

'Do you go for trips with your parents?' Inayat interrupted my thoughts.

'My father was in the army and died on field when I was very young. And now Mummy ... well ... she's been busy with her job. She travels a lot, which is why she sent me here.'

'I know the feeling, my mother is busy with her new husband, which is why she sent me here,' she said.

'I'm sorry,' I said.

'I wish I could take Nani Nana for a dive,' she said, changing the topic.

'And have you checked to see if you can't?'

'No.'

'But you must.'

'You're right. That could be our next trip, who knows. Maybe you could come with us?' she reached out and squeezed my hand.

And suddenly, in that moment, I wanted to ... I knew the feeling I had had all this while ... wanting to be around her all the time ... the knot I felt in my stomach when we were together ... how my heart raced around her ... I'd only ever felt this once before, with a boy, and this felt like a hundred times bigger. I wanted to hold Inayat ... to feel her close to me, to kiss her ... I liked Inayat, liked her more than a friend ... I liked a *girl* more than a friend.

'If you two don't join us now, you aren't getting any hot chocolate,' Ignaz shouted.

I laughed, kinda relieved about the distraction.

I couldn't do that. I couldn't like a *girl*. What would everyone think? I knew how often my friends made fun of the girls rumoured to be gay. I knew how those girls had been bullied in school. Of course, these were only rumours, but there was always an ... a rejection that these girls went through, and the giggles and whispers that followed them around school. It was brutal.

I wasn't a lesbian, was I? I couldn't be. I'd dated boys, kissed them, liked them. Not like how I did Inayat, never this strongly, no. God I wanted to kiss her so bad. I wanted to pull her closer, tighter against me, but I could almost feel the gaze of everyone around us and my mind telling me to stop. I was not going to be the person everyone singles out and leaves behind. I had spent too much time and energy to become who I am here today, stand where I did in school, so I got up to join the group instead.

'We'll talk more soon?' Inayat asked, smiling.

God, Inayat has a beautiful smile ...

Ugh. What was happening to me? Why was I feeling like this? I'd never felt like this before, not for anyone ... Even with boys I'd never felt this stupidly crushing. For weeks I had pretty much not let myself think about how I was feeling ... Liking a girl like this? It felt ... strange, and still I couldn't help myself. But I had to stop this. It wouldn't be right. I couldn't be this stupid.

I nodded hesitantly.

We spent the rest of the night playing games, exchanging notes on the gossip in school, and finishing all the food loot until we decided we really should go back before Miss Farzana woke up for her morning namaz and noticed us missing.

'Now that would be a fun ending to this night,' laughed Vrinda.

'Really man, ssssshhhh,' shushed Anjani.

CHAPTER 10

PEMA

'Aama's told me to give you these,' I said, taking a packet of khapse out of my bag and quickly hiding it in Inayat's desk before getting the rest. 'And these. She said she's like dried the meat out damn properly for the chebureki, so it shouldn't get spoilt soon, but she's asked you to keep it in a cool place and make sure to smell it before you eat to make sure it hasn't like gone bad. And this is sha balep, this can be stored like for some time and ...' I went on.

For those who have like no clue, these are Tibetan snacks, some of mine and Ina's favourites. They're like these puff pasty type things with the best, most insanely yummy meat fillings, especially how Aama makes them, slowly, 'letting the flavours stew over time on low flame' or something like that she says.

'Pema ... wait ... what's going on? Why ...'

I groaned. I had told Aama not to give me all this food. It could get so much attention, and like I knew Ina would have issues with it. Plus, I could get into trouble if the school people found out. We aren't allowed to bring any outside food to school. I mean, sure, that doesn't stop girls from hiding things in secret underwear pockets, distracting the matron while someone quickly drops a bag in a bush nearby to pick up later or other shit they can get away with, but still. Plus, all these packets Aama had given were like huge! Even with our desks right at the back of the class, I had to be so careful not to make too much noise. But Aama didn't listen, which was quite a shocker because how many times has the woman punished Dada and me for breaking the rules! Although I get it, I guess. Honestly, from the things my parents finally told me, I was totally worried for Ina too, so I was like oh my god, okay, have to. And Baba promised he would make sure I didn't have those chance frisks when getting into school. (Again, shocker!) Plus, if I was being completely honest, after the fight we had, I was kind of hoping this would make up a little.

'The Gorkhaland agitation ...' I whispered.

'What about it? And why the food?'

'Baba says it's all started already. Last evening, he called up Dada and told him to cancel his tickets back home for the summer holidays. And then Aama Baba locked me at home and went to the town to stock up on ration. And they came back with enough for like a hundred people.'

Ina continued to look at me with a 'I have so many questions and things to say' look, so I went on to tell her everything I knew.

'Umm ... They did tell me what was happening, said I can't not know now and stuff. I don't remember like everything, but okay, let me try. What Baba said was that after the whole compulsory Bengali policy thing, the local parties led a march to protest the ruling in a state meeting that was happening in town, but there was a clash or something with the police, and now the army has been called to control the protests. But things have gotten worse and the hill parties have decided to revive the demand for a separate state because they are tired of being like bullied and stuff.'

'And what are the repercussions of all of this?'

'I don't know, but Baba says there could be a strike, which is why like they've stored all that ration and Aama made this food for you. I'm sure the school will find like some sort of solution, but Baba says a bandh could mean that schools will be shut down too.'

And, I didn't say it, but it could mean all the girls have to go back home. But I don't even want to think about not seeing Ina every day.

I know I have said this a gazillion times now, but it's so unbelievable that I have to keep reminding myself of it. I have finally started to feel like I have an actual best friend, not something I made up in my head but a real one (even though she is friends with Nidra and all that and it still scares me, and I have to do my best to not think about it), and I can't imagine what would happen because of all this. Plus, we still haven't sorted out the whole fight we had the other day, and, who knows, maybe it will all end our friendship. And frankly like I think Baba is right. Ina really doesn't know anything about Darjeeling, and I don't get why she is so agitated about it. But maybe I shouldn't have said anything. I could have pretended to agree with her or something and then we would still have a chance of being friends because then there wouldn't be so many things that could break our friendship. I mean, is this whole agitation thing even that important? Over our friendship?

I know, my mind is amazing at catastrophizing (I learned the word after I realized I keep doing it all the time—cool no?).

Ina must have been talking to me all this time, because when my thoughts finally stopped, I saw her looking at me as if she was waiting for me to say something.

'Umm ...'

I think Ina has gotten used to these phases of mine, which is totally a sign of how good a friend she really is actually, because she like repeated herself without getting annoyed. 'I think you went into your thinking mode. Thank aunty for me, will you. And don't worry okay. From what I read, it always dies down. These people don't actually care beyond filling their coffers. And when that's done, well ... I know you don't believe me, and I'm so sorry I jumped to a conclusion about your life the other day. I've been thinking, and perhaps you're right, I don't know anything about any of this really and I might sound so tone deaf, but I do think that what your father is saying is blinded by his love for the town and the need for it to be better, which I understand. And perhaps a separate state would be right from everything you have said, I don't know, but it doesn't look like those leading the movement are thinking that, not as far as their trajectory goes.'

I know I shouldn't have said what I did next. I mean, fuck, I know like only two minutes ago I had thought I shouldn't have reacted the other day, but I did it again. 'I think my dad knows a little more than you. I mean, come on Ina, you are new here and you have only just found out about all this from what, a few books and newspapers? Plus, like, what do you gain out of this, and for us it could mean a lot. Shouldn't you be on my side?'

'Pema, I am on your side! My grandparents live in Hyderabad, and they've gone through this. They went through this when they decided to stay in India during the partition and were told how bad a decision it was. They know the difference between hollow, false promises and those with direction and deliberation. Maybe I'm wrong, Pema, but it doesn't feel like this person has direction. Maybe I'm plagued by what my grandparents have seen and experienced and I suppose it is stupid of me to say these things because I have never been affected by any of it at all. But I care for you. And even from the little I have read, history should have told us otherwise. This leader just doesn't sound honest, and the only ones losing will be the people, will be you.'

I could tell she was getting like triggered again, and I was damn annoyed at myself for not shutting up about this stuff. I wanted to, but like I literally couldn't stop myself. I was so conflicted between choosing Baba or her in this argument, and like I really got what Baba was saying. Plus, with Aama Baba talking about it so much and the whole town feeling almost like a war zone or something, it was really starting to scare me, and I just wanted all of it to end soon.

But before I could even like think about what to say next, again, we heard the clicking heels of Mrs Joshi and had to rush to hide all the packets of food and stare into our books—because for like all the 'this school has the best teachers from across the country blah blah blah' lecture Aama gives me, she would totally change her mind (yet again) if she had to attend one of Mrs Joshi's hour-long classes where she reads from the book, literally. I *could* do that!

Maybe if nothing works out I could consider becoming a lazy teacher in this school. My mind really has a pretty cool ability to multitask.

CHAPTER 11

INAYAT

God,
    I have never felt more alone, thanks to you.
    I miss Pema. She hasn't come the last two days, nor have any of the teachers from town. I suppose the agitation is heating up. We'd be fools to presume that any of this will end quickly. I can't imagine it ever does until plenty destruction is sought, innocence lost and the hunger for it all is squelched with enough money to last for some time at least. Although Sister Teresa hasn't spoken much of it in the assembly. She only said that we have nothing to worry about, that the school was not part of any political unrest, that they were taking care of it and we should focus on our schoolwork.
    But I haven't been able to focus at all. I miss Pema and her incessant chatter. I guess I've really gotten used to it. I'd started to feel less lonely with her around, even happier somehow. Although I might not tell her that myself. I remember that sleepover at Arshia's where we promised to be best friends, sisters even, and only a few weeks later all hell broke loose at home with Ammi and Abba. Is it bad to say hell? I forget. We were a happy family, for a while anyway, until Ammi found out about Abba's affair. All the signs were there—the night outs, the sleeping in the other room and talking into the wee hours of the night, the dressing up to work, the gifts we found in his drawer. But Ammi spent years telling herself and me that it was all in the head.

She never gave me the details of what really happened, but a part of me feels she was more embarrassed than hurt. A part of me believed her all those years when she said it was all okay. I wanted to. I really did love Abba, still do. He always took out time to do things with me while Ammi was busy working at college and around the house. I've been thinking of late, for all the resentment I have for Ammi, is it fair for us to hold our parents to such high moral standards? After all, it's their first time living too. Are you putting thoughts in my head so I will forgive Ammi?

Anyway, that was that. I was saying, I told Arshia and we had to leave shortly after.

And I remember my birthday with Nani Nana, Sidra Di, Manisha Ma'am and her husband at the club. Ammi was travelling for work, or so she said, so Nani Nana decided to throw me a dinner party. It was such a joyful evening, and I remember telling them how happy I was.

Well, only a few days later Ammi came back with Amir. And another few weeks later she told us they were getting married. Which brought me here. So, yes. I don't think I'm going to be telling Pema anything at all in case I jinx my whole life again. I should recite the ruqyah just to be safe.

It's funny how your ways work. To think only a few weeks ago I was happy being on my own and going from class to pottery to the dorm, and now I miss Pema. I can't help but feel afraid. And I think I may have already jinxed it all because we have had a few serious arguments about our differences as far as the agitation is concerned. I am not saying she's wrong in wanting and supporting what they are promising the locals. Theoretically it all makes sense, but from whatever little I have read and understood, there seems no credibility to these leaders. And I can't not tell her that. Or maybe she's right. Maybe I am insensitive and harsh, and an insufferable know-it-all the way I feel like I know everything about something I only learned of a few days ago. Maybe I'm wrong about all of it. What do I even know about any of this really, and who am I to tell them anything as an outsider? I was also terribly wrong in assuming that she didn't understand what being othered felt like. To think there is so much grief behind someone who gives so much love. I always thought her life was perfect. How wrong I was. I wish I could correct it all. I hope I can soon. Everything has been so rushed all this while, and the time's never felt right for us to sit and talk it out, but then I suppose there is no good time to say sorry, to fix things. You want me to live with the guilt of hurting my closest friend and learn from it, don't you? I think I would understand that intent.

But why is it that even Nidra has not been around? I see her in school and the house, but every time I try to speak with her she makes some excuse and rushes away. I don't know if it is something I did to her too. I can't think of anything really, and I've spent so many nights trying to dissect every single second we've spent together to find reason. We had such a good time at the lake that day, and we felt so close when we sat there ... it almost felt like ... like when Stephen Chbosky said, 'We didn't talk about anything heavy or light. We were just there together. And that was enough.' But she hasn't been around and I feel pained by it, pained and confused by how acutely it all makes me feel.

For weeks as we spent time together I knew I was feeling something I had never felt before, not for anyone. I have never had boys like me before, and I have never liked any either. But I know what I feel for Nidra seems a lot like how people around me speak about their boyfriends and girlfriends. All this time I refused to let myself unravel those feelings, but now that I have acknowledged what I feel, I don't want to stop feeling that. But you, you've taken that away from me too. Why? Because it's a sin for me to like a girl and I haven't stopped myself from it?

And you know the saddest part is—I have never been angrier at you, but I have no one else to speak to but you.

Ina.

CHAPTER 12

PEMA

Fuck fuck fuck fuck fuck. I want to cry so bad. Aama Baba are fighting, again.

They've been at it for like the whole week, and it's really scary, especially without Dada here. When all this started, they were just arguing, but now it's like full on fighting. I've never seen them like this. They've always been so cringe in love. Like those annoying cutesy couples in the movies. Dada and I were always telling them to stop being mush as hell in front of us. But now they are like shouting at each other, refusing to eat, sleeping in different bedrooms. It's completely nuts and so scary. I don't know what to do, whose side to be on and who to help at this point.

Baba wants to join the agitation. He thinks this time it will be different and he has to be part of it. Aama feels like completely unsafe about it. She is so scared she doesn't want any of us going out at all. She thinks there is no point anyways, that there are enough people to rally for this. Today she said something about how they are forcing people to donate and join the party and whatnot, and that really pissed Baba off. She's gotten on a whole different side of this whole thing, Ina's side almost.

Dada called today and told me that I've got to chill out, that I can't get affected by what they are doing between themselves.

'It doesn't look like they know what they are even saying to each other, Dada. I mean ...'

'Pem, they're worked up, and I get it. Things are really heating up. The party has announced an indefinite shutdown. God knows when things will open and what it all means. Thankfully Aama Baba stocked up on ration, but the tourist season will get affected, and because of it Aama's tea shop. And who knows if the school will pay Baba for this time off. Plus, there are all these fights around town. Some of my friends were telling me that people who aren't part of the cause are being harassed by the local parties, especially state government employees. And the army is not helping the situation.'

'But, Dada ...'

'They'll figure it out, naani. I'll speak with them. Why don't you just focus on covering the syllabus on your own. This is an important year.'

I was happy he was on a voice call and couldn't see my eyeroll, because then he'd annoy me about that too. I am so tired of these lectures. Every time I have like an opinion, I become a child, naani no naani yes, naani this naani that. I wish someone would ask me what I want, which is literally two things—for us to be safe through this and to go back to school to Ina. I don't think I've mentioned this, but every week she's taken out something like a minute from her seven minutes of phone time to call me. The first time I wasn't expecting it. I mean, we had all those fights about this stuff. And I slipped twice as I jumped over the pochcha from my bedroom to the drawing room when Aama yelled that it was Ina calling. I was damn excited. From the next time I just sat by the phone instead, with my feet up because, as Aama says, 'No one disturbs the pochcha.'

'Slowly, naani. She isn't going anywhere.'

Another lowkey eyeroll. Aama wouldn't understand.

'Watch your step. Look you've dirtied the floor. I just wiped it. Take off your slippers!'

Eyeroll count = three.

'He ... hello,' my heart was beating super fast as I picked up the receiver.

'Pem, hi!'

'Ina?'

'I thought I should call you. It was all so sudden, the shutdown and the school getting closed.'

'I know, Baba was saying that he doesn't expect it to be closed too long. I should be back soon.'

'I hope so.'

I smiled. *She misses me*, I thought. 'Have you all been having classes?'

'A few, with the resident teachers. Games have been cancelled because Sir Lama isn't in. So, we have some morning classes and then prep time in our dorms.'

'That must be nice no, being in bed all day?'

'Not really. I try go for pottery for a while every day. But the house girls have started a knitting challenge that keeps us going.'

'What kind of knitting challenge?'

Now I wanted to go to school so badly. I loved knitting and did it with Boju all the time! In fact, Boju had said my socks were so good that I could move on to vests now.

'Socks. The person who makes the highest number before the bandh opens wins one month of tuck coupons.'

'Oh.'

I think she could like tell that I was sad. Ina can be very like, like she can tell these things, because she said, 'Why don't you knit at home? I can ... I'll try tell Nidra that you are competing too.'

'Oh ya, you can tell Nidra.'

I had missed Ina and the school so much that I had completely forgotten about Nidra. But now that I thought about it, Nidra and Ina were probably spending a lot of time together now. *Who knows, maybe by the time I get back they will be like best friends and she won't care for me at all. Nidra is a lot of fun after all, plus super popular and stuff.*

'Hello? Hello Pema?'

'Uh ... oh ... yes, sorry.'

'I thought I'd lost you. But yes, start knitting.'

'Right ... okay.'

Suddenly her call didn't feel so great anymore. And knowing there was nothing I could do to change it made it just so much worse. It felt like old times all over again.

'Anyway, I thought I'd just check in, we didn't really get to say bye and talk about the whole argument we had.'

'It's okay, let's not talk about that now. And it's not really goodbye, no.'

'I know, okay. But you know what I mean.'

'Ya.'

I knew I was like really sucking at this chat, but I didn't know how to make it better.

'Okay, they're telling me to put the phone down now. I'll speak with you soon, Pema.'

'Oh okay. Yes, sure.'

'Take care.'

'You too.'

I put down the phone and ran back into my room while Aama screamed about how I don't help around the house and just keep rotting in my room. But I was feeling horrible and really didn't feel like being around anyone.

I want to like cry so bad all the time these days. First Aama Baba being crabby and taking it out on me. Second, and most of all, I didn't want to lose my best friend thanks to this stupid bandh; and with us not spending time every day and Ina having Nidra with her all the time, it could totally happen.

Had she asked me how things were at home? I don't think I even told her, and now I felt so stupid about it. It happens to me often. I get so nervous all the time. I start thinking so much about what to say and if I am saying the right things at all that I completely miss what the other person is saying, and then I have to make up something to make it sound like I was listening and that makes me sound even more stupid, sometimes even plain mean or snooty or something. And honestly now I really wish I *had* listened to Ina, because she would have actually heard what I had to say about things at home, unlike everyone else who thinks I am too young for all this. Damn, not a good day at all.

CHAPTER 13

INAYAT

God,

It all feels like a practical joke you're playing on me now. I can't seem to make sense of anything.

Sister Teresa called an assembly last evening to say that they're shutting down the school until the bandh is lifted. She said the parents were being informed and that the school would arrange for the students to be picked up as soon as possible.

And, ever since, the girls have been busy running from one block to the other, gathering all their things—clothes from one another, books from the classes, some even considerately distributing their tuck trunks amongst girls who aren't leaving immediately.

Ammi called today to say that she is going to come as soon as possible. She said Amir was unwell so she couldn't leave him immediately. I made the mistake of asking her what was wrong with him. Stomach infection. Stomach infection! I couldn't help laughing. I know it wasn't nice of me to laugh at someone's illness, and you must forgive me, but I couldn't help it.

Of course, she didn't take it well. She called me inconsiderate and heartless. Oh, and selfish. She said I'd hurt her immensely and I wanted to ask if she'd ever thought about how much she'd hurt me. There may have been other things she said, but my laugh had been replaced by disappointment by then and I didn't hear any of it. Am

I wrong in thinking that perhaps getting your daughter back home from a politically charged environment should be more important? Sure, Sister Teresa must have told Ammi that we were safe here and that there were other girls in the school, too. She reminds us of that every day. And I am not saying we aren't safe, and that the situation is dire; from the little we hear it is all happening in small bouts and skirmishes (if what we are being told is to be believed, which I don't entirely). Still, Amir is a grown man and can take care of himself, especially when everything is at his beck and call at the government posting. Shouldn't he tell her that he could take care of himself and that she should come get me home first? Shouldn't she be more concerned about me?

Then she wonders why I don't respond to her letters or calls. And Nani scolds me for not being nicer to her. And I feel guilty that you will think I am a bad person because I don't treat my mother with more love when you have told us she is our best companion, and the most deserving of our love and respect. Maybe I am just bitter about how much our relationship has changed and how distant I have felt from her over the last few years. Perhaps I need someone to blame for how I feel.

Not that I should complain about any of this. I would rather be stuck here than go to Ammi and Amir's place. I wish I could go to Hyderabad, but I wouldn't want Nani to stress over me when Nana isn't keeping too well.

I didn't even speak with her about this when I called, because, unlike Ammi, I knew she would worry endlessly. Although I'm sure they'll find out soon enough.

I think Nidra was convinced her mother would come immediately. She was one of the first to bring all her stuff from the class. But when I saw her in the mess later that evening, I could tell she was upset. And then it didn't matter that she refused to speak with me for whatever reason. I had started to deeply care for her, and with all her friends gone, I couldn't help but be concerned.

Which is why I ran up to her on our way back to the house and tried to cheer her up with my mother's excuse of being stuck tending to the infected stomach of her thirty-something new husband. And she laughed. I knew she needed someone.

'I suppose you'll want the packets of Indomie and Wai Wai that you distributed back now?' I asked.

'And the Jim Jams,' she laughed. 'Don't forget the Jim Jams.'

God, for her sake, let her mother come soon. And if you can at all, for mine, let my mother not come for as long as possible. Yes, I can hear Nani get very mad at me for saying this, and I know you will be too, but I am sure you know how I feel. I miss my mother too you know, just not the one I currently have.

So often I miss the time we were in Delhi, with Abba. I still remember the last picnic we went for to that bird sanctuary. Ammi and I went for a swim in the lake while Abba took photographs of the birds. And all three of us sat eating Abba's special burgers and chicken fingers—I slurped on a chocolate shake and Abba and Ammi on his special kesar chai. Ammi and I even fed some of the chicken fingers to the squirrels, something Abba said was really not great for them, but they seemed to enjoy it so much.

I am not saying that Ammi shouldn't have left Abba. I suppose she had to. But I do miss the old times, just the three of us, and I do miss Abba. We rarely ever talk anymore because Ammi refuses to let us. She made me promise I wouldn't talk to him. But now that I think about it, she didn't say I couldn't write to him. I suppose I could write to him from here! Would that be breaking my promise to Ammi? I'll have to sleep over it and ask Nani about it on our next call.

I guess the one partially good thing is that I think Pema and I are better. We still haven't spoken about our fight and fixed things. I would presume that we both still have the same stands, and I hate brushing things under the carpet—it never serves any good—but I guess for now just being able to talk a little must do. There is too much happening around us to pull us down anyway.

Ina

CHAPTER 14

NIDRA

I realize now that I run away from everything in my life that makes me uncomfortable. Which means I have actively avoided thinking about what's been happening in town over the last few weeks. As long as it didn't affect me, I didn't have to think about it beyond the lack of tuck, right? It's hard for me to think. Honestly, it's easier this way; especially now with my mum not coming to get me ASAP, I want to block it out completely. But I have to admit, having the school to myself has been *pretty* cool. I mean, okay fine, it's not really *all* to myself or whatever, there are still a fair few girls left. I think Sister Teresa mentioned twenty-something at breakfast today. But it still feels like it's all to myself. And Inayat. Having her around again has been incredibly nice actually.

Now that most of the students and staff have left, all the girls have been shifted to our block with Miss Ruth, who is too busy with her boyfriend to care about what we are up to. Ignaz always wished she was in Miss Ruth's block because it would make sending letters to her boyfriend and even sneaking in a cell phone so much easier. And I can now tell the charm in it, not gonna lie.

With no classes and routine, we get up late and make some breakfast in the block pantry. It's not much, usually some eggs, bread and milk, but we are allowed to sit in the common room, which means we get to watch TV while we eat, and that is always fun. We just started *13 Reasons Why*, and wow it's insanely creepy.

The teachers switch duties for the rest of the meals, and we usually eat in the mess with Sister Teresa and the few other nuns and staff who are still around. Miss Ruth also doesn't give a fuck about locking the pantry or any other door for that matter, which means most girls end up cooking up their stocks of noodles, coffee, hot chocolate and whatnot while having late nights in the dorms.

As for me, I spend most of my time with Inayat.

I avoided her for weeks after the party at the lake. I avoided everything I was feeling for her, ignored a part of me too I think. It felt easier, again. But with all my friends and most of the staff gone, I feel less scared about it all. I know it's crazy, being unable to be who you are with your own friends.

I'm beginning to realize that I have only been fighting how I'm feeling about Inayat because I am afraid of losing everything I have here. I've seen it happen before, how the judgement here can be ... it can be ... it can really break people. And I know when Mummy decided to get back to work after Papa passed away and I came here, it took me forever to be myself again and not have nightmares about being left all alone ... unloved, unaccepted, I don't know. I don't think I want to feel any of that again. But Inayat makes me happy. And that day, when Mummy told me she couldn't come, Inayat being around really helped. It's like the weeks of silence never existed. I don't know why Inayat wasn't mad at me. I think I would be if I were her. But we didn't even talk about it, just fell right back to where we were, better now actually because I don't have to worry about the others anymore. Although I still can't seem to get rid of those knots in my stomach, but I suppose I'm not trying to right now anyways.

Inayat is quite serious about her exams next year, so she spends her mornings studying while I go to the music room to play a bit of the keyboard and practice my dance.

In the afternoons, after lunch, we often sit and read in the library. She's getting me hooked onto some of the books she's reading, which is kinda cool actually. Feels like our thing. My last was *Tomorrow*

There Will Be Apricots. Ina and I were talking about our mothers and she told me about this one. She said that the relationship between Lorca and her mother reminded her of her own, how it made her realize that a wall had formed between her mother and her over the last few years. I could see her tear up when she told me about how she's spent so much time walking on eggshells around her mother, trying to win her love while she was crumbling herself ever since her parents split. Honestly, I couldn't help but feel grateful for my mother, despite all my resentment of how little time she gives me. And although I completely get what she means by wanting to please your mother all the time, I couldn't even imagine what she was going through until I began reading the book. I swear, every page had me wishing I could hold her and tell her it would be okay. And I think she sensed that it was tough for me too, because she decided that we should move to a mush John Green novel after which I quite enjoyed.

Anyways, in the evenings, she teaches me how to do pottery.

But there really isn't anything like the nights at school.

With the pantry open to us, and Miss Ruth not giving two fucks about lights out, Inayat and I often fill a thermos with hot chocolate and a hot case with some noodles to take to the hill by the mess from where you can see the entire town light up at night. Today we took two blankets and laid one out to sit on and one to cover ourselves and just stayed there for hours, me reading this mystery by J.K. Rowling and her finishing her journaling. Inayat even made me a special biscuit cake, layered with crushed Bourbons, followed by the Bourbon cream, Jim Jams with the jam centre, Jim Jam cream and melted Dairy Milk icing topped with M&Ms.

'This is so good!' I declared, putting down the book for a sip of the hot chocolate.

'I started with *Silkworm*, which is the second, but it's better to start with this I think,' Inayat said, looking up.

'Yes, this one is great! Is it true J.K. Rowling got uncovered or whatever as the author of this? That her cover was blown?' I asked.

'Well, sort of. *The Sunday Times* revealed it first. They claimed that they got these two professors … what were their names?'

'I really don't care, I promise. I won't remember them anyway,' I chuckled. 'Go on.'

'Oh okay,' Inayat smiled. 'So yes, they said they got these two professors to run language analyses on the novel and the previous works of Rowling to find out, but turns out this lawyer who worked for Rowling told his wife who told a friend who told the reporter on Twitter or something. Can you believe it!'

'Well, gossip chain and whatnot I suppose.'

'Rowling didn't feel so. She said she wanted to stay anonymous for some time longer because she felt like having the pseudonym of Robert Galbraith was liberating.'

'What rubbish, I am sure it helped sell the book so much more.'

'I suppose. It apparently got rejected too.'

'Imagine, they must have sacked the editors who read it.'

Inayat laughed. 'And Rowling went through all the trouble of making up a story about the pseudonym and how it was to protect the identity of the government official in the Royal Military Police.'

'I mean, she's good at making up stories I suppose!'

We laughed, me at the irony of how much I understood Rowling's need to stay hidden, even when, for the first time in a long while, I was feeling an ease of being completely myself I've only ever felt when dancing.

'Here, it's almost over,' I said, handing over the thermos of hot chocolate to Inayat. 'You know we are on our last box of hot chocolate powder.'

'That should last a few more cups, right?'

'Yes. And Nitisha gave me some of her instant caramel coffee mix sticks. So that should do I suppose.'

'Pema's khapse!'

'What?'

'I just remembered. Pema's mother had sent me her homemade khapse, chebureki, sha phaley and some other things. Pema brought them some time ago and I loved them, so when the news of the agitation was doing the rounds, her mother made lots of them for me.'

'That's so nice of her. She's a really sweet girl; she's always around to help with the house stuff whenever I need it. My friends aren't like this, or like you. They're ... I don't know ... they're a lot of fun, but I've been feeling ... I don't know ... they can be tough sometimes, especially when they don't like you. And I can't talk to them about everything,' I said.

'Hmm. Yes, Pema is very nice. She's made life here a whole lot easier,' Inayat said softly. 'But I have to ask, why are you friends with these girls if you feel this tentative about them? Shouldn't you be able to be yourself with your friends and enjoy it?'

'Oh, I don't know. We've been friends for a long time, and I've never really thought about it,' I lied. Truth was, I'd not let myself think about it, and it was never targeted at me, so it was easier to not be bothered by it.

'You like brushing things under the carpet, don't you?' Inayat chuckled.

I laughed. 'I suppose so, although I never realized I was doing that until recently. I guess it's easier that way. I don't like change. But anyways, is there any of this loot left? And where is it?'

'You're doing it again!' she exclaimed. 'And no, Pema gave it to me in class, but Mrs Joshi walked in as she did, and we were so rushed that I slid everything under the books and forgot about it.'

'And these are books you haven't touched in the last few days? How is that possible?!' I joked.

'I hope the food is not spoilt.'

'Come on now, let's go get it.'

'But the class block must be locked at this hour.'

'But Miss Ruth has all the keys and, if I am not wrong, it's Friday, which means Zoom date night with her boyfriend. We could sneak them from her room!'

'We couldn't!' Inayat exclaimed.

'Don't be a chicken! It'll be fine. We could complete the mission in fifteen minutes tops if you don't spend more time thinking about it.'

And we did. It was chill enough. With little to look out for, we were in the class block and back to the dorm in, yup, less than fifteen minutes, the food under our sweaters and in good shape. And I swear it turned out to be so lucky for us, because, over the next few days, our meals started to get smaller—we were told that we had to ration because of the limited groceries the school was being able to get—and the tuck trunks we had, including what the other girls had left us, started to get wiped out insanely quickly.

CHAPTER 15

INAYAT

Dear God,

I want to understand your ways. I suppose someday I will. Why you do what you do, why you keep us from things our hearts most desire. Nani keeps saying I lack tawakkul, that it is the most integral sentiment in my relationship with you and I must work to cultivate complete faith in your plan. And it's not like I don't have faith. But I think, unlike Nani, you feel like a friend to me, my best friend in fact, which is why I write to you every day, because I like telling you about my day, complaining to you about everything I feel is going wrong and showing gratitude for things that are joyous. I guess I write to you to make sense of what is happening around me when I don't know what is happening most of the time. And because most of the time I have needed someone to talk to and I haven't always had that. Maybe in between all of the thinking and wondering and asking I get mad and even question you, but is it wrong to do that with your best friend? It's not that I don't believe it all will work out in a way that I will come to be grateful for. I know you can move things for my duas to come true. I do trust that my prayers will see fruition, or at least you will teach me to make my peace with it and even share some great happiness in the process (like I did in Hyderabad). But ever so often something happens and I am left wondering if I'll have the former.

Like with Nidra. I'm not angry with her for not speaking to me those weeks. I suppose, if she felt even a smidgen of what I felt, it might have been difficult for her to understand what was happening. I still can't make sense of my feelings for her, and I think I'm also struggling with what the my faith says about it. But I don't want to. I like how I feel about her, and, if I really listened to my heart, even my gut, I know I wouldn't mind if we became more than friends. In fact, I would like it. And isn't it you who puts these feelings in our hearts? It's such a cliché, but it feels like it fits, you know. When I'm with her, it feels like I believe in your will so much more, like you've got it all figured out for me, and I feel excited to see how life unfolds. Could it really be a sin to feel like this? To feel anything that brings me closer to you?

I want to believe Nidra feels the way I do about her too. Although there are days when she's extremely sullen. Her mother hasn't come yet, and even though she hasn't said anything to me, I know every time her mother calls Miss Ruth she rushes down, hopeful that it will be the day she says she is coming. She misses her mother so much; I know she does. She tries to hide it, she smiles a lot and rambles about silly things, but her face gives it all away.

And it happened again today. Her mother called to say that she wouldn't be able to come for at least another week because the project for which she was in the UK was stuck at a crucial juncture. I guess I understand it better than my mother's excuse, which has now moved on from Amir's stomach infection to his work crisis. But nevertheless, Nidra was very upset, as opposed to me who was happier here than I could ever be with my mother in Lucknow. It must be nice to be so close to your mother that you are angry about being apart. I remember feeling that way a long time ago, and I really miss it.

Anyway, Nidra didn't want to talk today, so I let her be.

I know how I feel when I'm upset. Times when I feel like there is nothing anyone can say that will help, I just want to be left alone too. Although, for how lonesome I like to be, I am never bothered having Nidra around, no matter the mood. But I really did want to do something unlike me, something fun, like Nidra would do, something that would really cheer her up. After all, over the last few months, she's brought me more happiness than I'd felt in forever, and it's never been in ways I would have expected.

So I decided to plan something different from our usual graveyard shenanigans, something we would have to break maybe a hundred school rules for, not to mention if it would even be possible or safe in the town chaos, something so stupid that would take her mind off things completely, something I needed Pema's help to execute seamlessly. And while Miss Ruth was drying her hair in the sun, I snuck into her room and used her computer (I remember Nidra speaking with Ignaz about her password being Shiven, after her boyfriend) and left Pema a quick DM about what I had in mind—a late night stroll out in the town.

'Can be done for sure. We just have to pick the right track,' she replied. 'How will you manage to get out though?'

'Leave it to Sister Mary,' I smiled as I wrote. The heart can make us do strange things, really.

'Okay, Lover's Road. Meet me by the abandoned tea shack. 10 p.m. Wear black.'

Before I could react to the realization that I had unwittingly dragged Pema into a plan that could potentially prove disastrous, she had left a thumbs up and logged out.

I don't know what I am doing. I know it's beyond reckless. Maybe I've completely lost my mind. And now I've got Pema involved too. But with each passing day I see Nidra battling her sadness alone and I really want to do something to help. Of course, now I can't abandon this even if I want to seeing as Pema will be waiting for us out there. I just hope what she has said about the agitations being limited to the centre of town is true. Please let this be a success, protect us.

Yours, Ina

CHAPTER 16

PEMA

I was excited as hell. I'd gone completely nuts in the past like whatever weeks imagining I'd lost my friend—journaling about it, playing pretend situations where there'd be like a new girl who comes in and we'd become best friends and then Ina'd be like insanely sad about it and she'd try to win me back and whatnot. But Ina's DM was like ... I don't know ... like I smiled and felt lighter or something even though I only later realized what I'd gotten us into with the bandh. I mean, I was pretty sure nothing was happening this side, although not like I could back out now even if it was because Ina would be waiting there at Lover's Road. But yay! Ina would be there! I was so so so happy ... until I saw her come down the road, with *her*.

What the actual fuck.
Why was she here?
Why had Ina not told me?
This was meant to be like our thing.
Ina waved at me.
This is not the time to think about these things, I told myself. *There will be plenty of time for it later, in my long lonely life at home.* I tried really hard to shut my brain off and waved back.

'Hey,' I whispered.
'Hi,' Ina said, giving me a hug.

I smiled at her. She looked completely herself. *Is it possibly that this is all like in my head?* But I didn't have time to figure it out.

'Hi Pema,' Nidra smiled.

I gave her a tiny smile back.

'So, what do you have in mind?' Ina asked.

I hesitated. My plan was to sneak out once Aama Baba had gone to their rooms and take Ina for a walk through Lover's Road. I had told her all about like how Baba and I go down there in the mornings to watch the sunrise. Of course, Baba doesn't know, but Dada and I often come here at night. On like a cloudless night it feels like you can see the entire Milky Way or something. It's ridiculously pretty. Dada and I lie down on this clearing type thing in the middle of the track, him smoking his joint and telling me about the different constellations, and me trying not to like sleep off because he can be such a geek with all his astronomy stuff. Dada's favourite is Orion, because apparently you can like see it practically all the time or whatever. The lamest reason really. Mine, I've decided, is Lyra. It's named after a stringed musical instrument, lyre, that this one Greek mythology musician used to play. But I don't like it because of that. That's all boring random stuff. So Lyra isn't like a big constellation or anything. In fact, it's the fifty-second. But it has Vega, which is the fifth biggest star in the sky, and the second biggest in the northern hemisphere. And that feels like totally my constellation. I mean, it's not the biggest or the brightest, in fact it's rather small, like me, but it has this one special thing, which doesn't make it the most special thing in the world or anything, but like special enough. I'd like to be that you know—special enough somewhere.

Anyways, I have gotten totally distracted again. I was saying, I had told Ina about all this and wanted to show her some of the stuff today. I guess not the constellation, because it was one of those like typical gloomy, foggy, rainy Darj days and we'd be lucky to even see a peek of the moon. But I was hoping to take her to the spot where Dada and I lie (I imagined us lying there and telling each other our deepest secrets, swearing to lifelong secrecy; we'd even pluck some of the wild daisies I wanted to show her the first day and play the question game) and then all of the special ones I have with Baba. There is the place with the yellow flowers that we pick and pop on each other's heads, and this other one that has these sour green leaves that Baba taught me to peel and eat with salt and chilli (I was carrying some of it in my pocket, along with a forgotten joint of Dada's I thought we could try. Dada says he's not opposed to me trying as long as I do it under his supervision after I turn eighteen. But I thought it might be fun with Ina, and I had heard of some girls in my tuition try it and figured it couldn't be all that bad or anything). And then there's this cave of sorts that leads to a tiny spring with powdery, purple-coloured wildflowers growing around it that is kind of really pretty.

There's more, but today was definitely not the day for it. I would take them through the Lover's Road and that'd be about it.

'Well, the Lover's Road goes down this way. I thought we could take the walk down,' I said.

'This looks seriously adventurous,' Nidra commented.

Ina laughed.

She didn't feel like that shy Ina in class or around other people in school. *She must be like really comfortable with Nidra*, my mind concluded.

'Come on, it should be fun. This is the walk Baba and you take, right Pem?'

She remembered.

I smiled a little. 'Yes. It'll be fine, Nidra. Let's go. It isn't like a hard trek; it only looks like it is. It is pretty easy actually. Just avoid this garbage dump. I've slipped into it once and I swear I smelled like poop for a week. And, of course, be careful at the broken stone bridge. You have to make sure you don't slip on the moss-covered stones. Because there is a jhora that runs under it and the only way up will be once you've reached the river.'

'Jhora?'

'Oh, it's this manmade stream of sorts that steers the rainwater to the river.'

'What!'

'And you should also warn her about the small patch of vines that we have to cross that has those tiny snakes you told me about. They're harmless, right Pema?' Ina winked at me.

'Huh? Oh ya ya, totally chill, Baba says. They only leave you with like a burning rash that lasts a few days, nothing scary poisonous or anything.'

'But other than these two things it should be fine.'

'Ya ya, totally.'

You know how you read about it in books all the time—the colour drained from her face and whatnot—I saw it for the first time on Nidra.

Ina burst out laughing, and so did I.

We felt like a team, Ina and I. And I immediately felt better about the whole situation.

'Hey! That was mean,' Nidra said, slapping both of us hard on our backs and pushing us down the narrow path to Lover's Road.

I refused to show them my spots. And Ina didn't ask about them either, I guess because she possibly got that I didn't want to with Nidra. But the walk was fun anyways. We walked one after the other, Nidra literally yell-singing na na na na na na na, na na na na na na na, na na na na na na na, na na na na na na na (you know, from that Ranbir and Deepika movie where he has this superhuman thirst for adventure until love tames him or something, but let's be real they would have gotten divorced like in two years of marriage anyways? No? Okay, never mind), but it didn't really make much sense to be honest. I mean, I might have sung *Madagascar* songs considering Lover's Road is like this super narrow muddy path in the middle of a scary dense forest along the edge of a hill, but okay, I'll give it to Nidra, her choice was kind of chill too.

'You want some bun-chop and piro aloo?'

It was kind of a windy day, and there was this like cold, misty dew left from the rain that had poured all afternoon, which I weirdly love a lot. Everyone hates Darjeeling in the rains; it's muddy and mucky and inconvenient and stuff, but I absolutely love it. I love it because it comes with the mist, which makes me feel, well, less lonely, and makes it impossible to think, which I kind of need often. It's so dense, the mist, you can hardly see anything ahead or around and like I can just bury my nose in it, and it tingles and goes all red, and I can keep going, as if hand in hand, less lonesome, happier even. This with a warm snack of my favourites would be a pretty good ending to this above-average-but-still-room-for-improvement outing.

'At this hour?' Ina asked.

'I would love some!' Nidra raised her hand.

I laughed.

'Yes, at Woodstock café,' I said.

'A café?'

'I mean, to be real it's not a café or anything. More like this wooden shack on a hilltop overlooking a ginormous cemetery. They have a super tiny burner for all the cooking and short wooden stools to sit on; and you have to use the ground or your hands for a table. But don't say that to Joey Uncle. He's the owner and like kind of cool, but loony. If you dare to ask him about his day, he tells everyone about how he starts his day with "a gargle of Debussy, a breakfast of Tchai ... Tchaikovsky, a lunch of Chopin, a dinner of Stravinsky, and a drink of Joni Mitchell". They're all some music composers who made romantic melodies and something about the night or some other weird rubbish, I don't know, I've just had to sit through too many of these endless convos between Dada and Joey Uncle and focus on the food as much as possible. It's ridiculously annoying, but Uncle makes the best bun-chop and aloo. And butter tea. Yum! So, I guess it is worth it. Except that one time when both of them made me literally write down the names of these musicians so I would remember and would not give me anything to eat until I got them right.'

'Okay, sold. I like Joey Uncle!' Nidra laughed.

'But will it be open with the agitation?' Ina asked.

'He opens from the side and like refuses to stop his business. Refuses to close. He's writing a new song about it too apparently, how music and bun-chop are the soul's soup or something.'

We laughed together. And for some time then it felt like we were all kind of best friends. *But, in a group of three best friends, wouldn't there always be two who are closer? And what happens with the one who is singled out?* my mind wondered. *Obviously, you in this one.*

I shook the thought off and told them to follow me to the side door.

Oh, and I'm guessing you'd wonder how we could be walking around in town like this, chill as hell, while the agitation is going on. Well, the mist. You've got to the love the mist. Plus, like I was saying the activity is mainly around the centre of town, the busier side where all the government buildings are, and the markets. Lover's Road is a like in the middle of the jungle and, as Ina would say, no one would care about it because there's no 'real gain' from it or anything. Or so I had hoped when I made the plan.

Anyways, back to it.

We knocked. And Joey Uncle opened the door.

'Ah! Dichen's sister. Come for a midnight snack?' he said. You could see his disappointment when he figured Dada wasn't with me. Like I need more of that negative self-talk, I mean, really. But he quickly got us all a plate of bun-chop and aloo to dip in, no questions asked, left our chais in the pot and asked us to serve ourselves while he went back to his seat by the window with his cat, Mouni, and the Walkman.

'What next, Pema?' Nidra asked after licking her plate clean and taking seconds.

'Well … tea anyone?' I said, pouring it into three cups. 'We could go to …'

'Shouldn't we head back to school now? It's past eleven,' Ina interjected.

'But the bungalow isn't too far from here. We could go see it, and then like you guys could go from there?' I was so not ready for the outing to end.

'A haunted house?'

I laughed. 'More like an abandoned British bungalow that I've always wanted to check out. People say it's haunted, but I don't know if it is really.'

'I think we should stay longer and explore this bungalow,' Nidra nodded.

'Outvoted!' I shouted. And was almost glad Nidra was there.

We quickly finished our tea and said goodnight to Joey Uncle (who didn't even bother to look up, might I add), and made our way up the hill and then down another like narrow jungle path that opened out into this ... I don't know what the English word is, but we call it chowr ... this open field of sorts I suppose ... and that is where the bungalow stood.

'Oh. Not the old regal British bungalow I was expecting,' whispered Nidra.

We giggled.

It's true, the bungalow was not like pretty or anything. In fact, I guess I described it completely wrong when I called it a bungalow. It looked more like a hostel or hospital type place—boxy, a rectangular building with three or four floors, rooms in a row one after the other and a corridor running in front connecting all of them. What I liked was the windows that covered most of the building in the front, so many of them broken by the local boys to 'let the ghosts escape' or whatever. And I was insanely curious about how like silent this place was, like it had really ancient secrets and it was making sure you left it alone and didn't come in to find out. And it got even spookier in the mist. Oh, and I loved loved loved the spiral staircase on the side that went all the way up.

'Well, what are we waiting for? Let's go in,' said Nidra.

I nodded.

'I don't know,' said Ina, 'it doesn't feel right to break in.'

'Ina, we aren't breaking in. It's an abandoned house. And look, the door is already broken into,' Nidra said.

Ina ... she called her Ina. That's what I call her. I was getting jealous again. And I know I would have felt it longer had Ina not taken my hand and nodded to say okay.

'Okay,' Nidra said.

We walked together to the bungalow, through the front door and into the corridor.

'Which way should we go?' Nidra asked.

'I mean, straight?' I said.

Nidra and I laughed, looking at the one dark corridor in front of us.

'Ssshhhh,' Ina said.

You could hear all of us breathe loudly in the spooky silence. And for all the excitement we had (or at least Nidra and I did) about adventuring into an abandoned and possibly haunted bungalow, I could tell that as soon as we were in, with the wind whistling between the broken windows and the creaky doors, and the drying leaves crunching under every step, we were shit-our-pants scared.

'Let's just ...'

But a rustle stopped her in the middle.

'Okay, really let's get out. Now,' Nidra whispered.

She reached out to grab my hand and me Ina's, and we were hurrying out, from the other side this time because we had completely lost track of where we were, when a shadow blocked our path.

'Who are you?'

'Umm ... fuck ... I ... we ... umm ... fuck,' I stammered.

'You girls can't be here,' the shadow hissed, opening the door to a room and pushing us in. I had completely totally lost my voice, and I'm guessing Ina and Nidra had too, because I didn't hear a word from them as the shadow (which was obviously a man) pushed us through the room and into another one at the back.

We're going to die. We're so going to die.

'You're going to wait here with us until we are sure the coast is clear. We don't know who you may have tracked with you.'

As our eyes got used to the darkness and the dim light coming from a candle, we saw the room, more like broom closet we were in, and we finally saw the face of the shadow who honestly looked just as scared as us.

Oh god, I've gotten Ina and Nidra into a hostage situation.

He gestured for us to sit, and I noticed a lady and two children sitting huddled together on a tiny mattress in the corner.

'Baba,' the girl said, reaching out for the man's hand, and for the first time in like forever, the three of us felt a little calmer. The father, on the other hand, continued to look angry.

'Stop it now, Anil,' the mother said, 'they're just young girls.'

'And I am wondering what these *young girls* are doing here, Rani.'

'Umm ... we ...' Ina stammered.

'Well, we wanted to explore the bungalow ...' said Nidra, who seemed to have gotten her voice back.

'These aren't times to go exploring,' he cut her off. 'It isn't safe, not for you and definitely not for us. Now how long has it been since you were out there?'

Ina squinted at her watch. 'About seven minutes?'

'But I thought this was an abandoned bungalow,' I continued, getting more curious now that I felt safer. 'What are *you* doing here?'

'That's none of your business,' the father snapped.

'Anil.' The mother put her hand on his shoulder to calm him down.

'No, they could be spies. He's got plenty of young people working for him.'

'They hardly look like the kind, Anil. And if they had to be, the men would not have been far, would they?'

She told us what they were doing there. How they were government employees and had to go into hiding because the young members of the current ruling party were burning the houses of anyone and anything related to the central government. How they had been hiding in a toy train museum that was burnt down only recently without much thought about its historical value. How they felt unsafe anywhere in town. And because they couldn't leave or ask someone for help, and there seemed to be no neutral person, party or organization to go to, they had come here. She cried as she talked about the almost-over rations and the risk of being holed up in this place for god knows how long.

I couldn't help but think about everything that was wrong with this whole situation. I mean, innocent people stuck in this bungalow, actually in this tiny-ass claustrophobic closet with god knows what food, with their kids, while we were like completely nuts looking at this as an adventure. How stupid and blind were we, or rather me.

'We'll come back and bring you some ration,' Ina said. 'Wait, here, I have this packet of biscuits I carried from school.'

The man tried to stop us, but the children quickly took the biscuits and gobbled them up.

'No, you just get out of here and don't come back. In fact, I think it should be safe for you to leave now,' the father said sternly.

'Anil,' the mother implored. 'Some ration might be nice.'

'No, Rani.'

But I saw Ina give a small nod to the mother and knew what she was thinking. 'Thank you,' she whispered. 'Really, if there was anyth—'

'No,' the father said again, pushing us out of the house, and looking around before nodding for us to leave.

We quietly made our way back up the hill and through Lover's Road to where we had met, still taken aback by what had just happened. I know I was shivering, and it was definitely not the cold.

'We'll see you again, okay Pema?' Ina said.

'Yes, this was fun, for a while at least anyways. Thank you,' Nidra agreed.

I smiled, but only a little, now realizing that the two would leave, together again, and I would be left here, alone. Again.

'Yes,' I said, giving both of them a hug. 'See you soon, promise.'

CHAPTER 17

INAYAT

God,
    Before I even begin to word vomit about everything that happened today, because there really is so much I need to put down to make sense of it all for myself, I need you to make sure Pema is back home and safe. Please take care of her. She's all alone and out in the middle of who knows what and I'm so scared.
    There have been plenty of times in my life that I have looked back on and thought to be fleeting, a blur of surreal joy or dissected grief. Today I can't even put a label on the whirlwind I feel inside of me. I almost can't feel my insides at all. It was the most horrendous reality check, as if what we had experienced on our first night out was not awful enough—to see an innocent family have to resort to hiding, and in such dingy quarters at that, with nothing to eat—it made me hurt so terribly to think of the injustice they'd suffered. Over the years I have had a lot of complaints for you, but even amidst those complaints I knew that I was taken care of, that you had enough people around me to make sure I was comfortable, and safe. But this family felt all alone.
    Which is why I was determined to go back with food. I knew Uncle wouldn't be happy, but in that short exchange with Aunty, I had promised her that I would be back, and I had to.
    So, in the evening, I went to Nidra to tell her what I had in mind in case she came looking for me.

'I will come along.'
'It could be risky.'
'I can take a little risk for another round of that bun-chop.'
I laughed but asked her to let me go on my own. She dismissed it.
'So, break into the mess to see what we can find?'
Nidra had done it plenty of times to know her way around the place. Of course, nothing had prepared us for the dismal sight of the mess pantry. I suppose we can often complain about being treated as kids, but one of the perks is how shielded we can be from things. I had tried to keep up with what was happening in town with my calls to Pema and the measly little that the news covered on TV. We knew that the rations were slim—the meals at school had come down to runny dal, veggies and small portions of rice or roti—but in the pantry it looked scarcer than it did on our plates.
'We can't take this, it wouldn't be right,' I had said.
'I promise I will eat a toast less and let go of my cereal.'
'I will too.'
So we picked up a packet of bread and filled up a zip lock with cereal. Of the little tuck we had left, we took the kids all the chocolates and candies. Nidra even gave her last packet of Jim Jam.
I left Pema a DM—someone should know what we were doing—but she immediately replied 'Lover's Road, 10p.m.' I got no reply to my message telling her to stay home because it might not be safe.
When we got to Lover's Road, Pema was waiting behind the abandoned tea shack. There was little talk as we made our way across. There was purpose in our strides and a weird feeling in my stomach that we had to get there and get out soon. You tell us to trust our gut, and perhaps I should have heard mine, but I was led by a strong need to help them, and I was sure my intention was honest enough to carry us through.
I guess it was, in the end. I am hoping it was anyway, and that Pema got home safe.
We got to the bungalow in no time, and I promised Nidra we would stop at Woodstock on our way back.

In the bungalow, we crept in and knocked at the door to draw attention—anyone trying to break in wouldn't. And in no time we saw Uncle's shadow appear at the door.

'What the hell are you girls doing here again?' he whispered, though I could tell that if he could he would have much rather shouted at us at the top of his lungs.

'We ... we,' I was stuttering, so Nidra finished my sentence.

'We wanted to get you some food,' she said, extending the bag.

He hesitated before taking it. Often, when you have been treated unfairly, you become incapable of understanding and accepting the kindness that you may receive after. And from the little Aunty had told us that day, they had been pushed into this hole for no fault of their own, simply because of the mad clashes between those high up. So I was not shocked by his behaviour at all.

'Oh ... um ... that's kind ... but this still isn't right, safe, coming here ...' he stammered.

What happened next is the part I can't recall or make sense of.

I remember Pema knocking me in my ribs, only because they still hurt, and pointing at the chowr where some men were coming down with blazing torches. And I remember telling Uncle to run and hide, that I could stall them for some time. I could tell that the men knew there was someone in the bungalow, otherwise there was no reason for them to be there, and as far as I was concerned, they could think it was me.

'Pema,' I had shouted, 'go!' pointing in the direction we had come from. And I grabbed Nidra's hand and made a run for it in another direction. I thought it would help to divide them.

I don't know how long we ran for, but I remember looking back and seeing some of the men follow us for a long while. I didn't know where we were or where we were running to, just that we had to keep going.

It's all a haze now.

I don't think I thought about you at all in that time, or that you would take care of me, but I guess I should have known that you would. Because there is no other way that ... Wait, I think I can hear Nidra call me. I'll write soon.

CHAPTER 18

PEMA

I knew the cave was not too far away and possibly my best bet for a hideout. It was covered in these thick shrubs and practically invisible to anyone who wasn't looking carefully. And considering these men looked like so pissed and hot headed, they would miss the biggest clues, forget small ones like these. Any other place I could think of was either too far away or too dangerous in the rain.

So I ran, like, damn, I don't remember ever running like that ever before. I mean, almost every year I run the 100, 200 and 400-metre races for the house games, but not because I *can* actually run. It's mostly because I *have to*, because we usually don't have enough runners, and you get participation points so you can't not have someone run. Story of my life, no? I am the two participation points. LOL. But I swear this time I ran like I was born to run.

Of course, I had like no idea what I was running from. As soon as I heard Ina scream I bolted and didn't look back. My first thought was to go to Joey Uncle's, but that would have put him at risk and obviously I couldn't do that. The next was the cave, and without like any doubt to follow it I ran to it and sat there for god knows how long. I swear, every creak of a leaf made my heart pound like crazy, and every wind whoosh made me pray the hardest I ever had. It was damp in the cave, which I hadn't noticed before, and for the first time I noticed the sound of the spring. It was kind of calming actually, almost. And I tried to focus on it for a long time before creeping out and making my way back home and in through my bedroom window. A quick check around the house and I knew everything was fine. Aama Baba were still asleep and totally oblivious. Phew. This had all been completely stupid, so so stupid of us now that I think about it. But anyways.

I know I've probably said this like so many times before, and I probably will again, but seriously, I don't think I can really describe how I felt between the time I heard 'run' to when I heard both my parents snoring in their separate bedrooms (yes, now it was cold war). I had made it back home safe, and I felt like crazy relieved. For a minute anyways, because it quickly went away at the thought of Ina and where she was.

I immediately turned on my computer and logged into my email. The only way to get in touch right now would be a DM.

'Hi.'
'Are you there?'
'What happened?'
'Have you reached okay?'
'You and Nidra.'
'…'
'Hello?'
'…'

I walked around my dark room shitting my pants, looking at the dimly lit screen, the cursor on the chat blinking like my heart waiting for a reply.

I kind of remember there being three men, and I know that at least one of them followed me for a little. I have no clue what happened to him, but I knew Ina and Nidra were chased too. And they went up the other side, where there was literally no place to hide in the mess of like construction and houses, unless they broke into a house or something. Or possibly they went down the cemetery and then the tea estate. That might have made a better escape route … not that they knew of it, plus that would only get them ridiculously far away from the school.

I really should have gone with them, I thought. *You don't say,* my mind mocked. *Stupid. Stupid. Stupid.*

'Hi.'

I woke up to the ping.

'Oh my god, hi. Are you okay?'

'Yes. We got back to the school. Nidra just came to tell me that Miss Ruth was out strolling so I rushed to DM you.'

'I was very worried.'

'Did you get back okay?'

'Ya. I hid for a bit and then ran home.'

'Oh my.'

'What about you?'

'I don't remember clearly, but I was just …'

'Writing in your diary, go on.'

'Well, yes. We ran for a while up the hill. And the men followed us. I was certain they would catch up and do something bad to us, but I didn't want to think of it, Pem. So we kept running as fast as we could. But the hill was steep and we got tired soon. Luckily, the men did too I suppose, because even though we were dragging ourselves they didn't seem to catch up. It felt like we would fall down dead, we were so out of breath. That's when this lady in a house close by motioned to us. Considering we would have fainted soon enough and the men would have caught up with us anyway, we had little choice but to go in.'

'What the fuck, Ina. I mean, I get it I guess, but that's still crazy!'

'Well, it was either her or the men, wasn't it. Anyway, she was a godsend. She let us hide at hers until we saw the men trudge up looking angry and confused and we were certain the coast was clear. She had worked with the local party, you know.'

'That can't be safe, Ina. Did you tell her anything?'

'We told her that we were there to explore the bungalow when the men came at us. She might have thought we were complete fools, but she didn't say a word. She did tell us about how she had been one of the men. How she was part of the agitation in the 1980s and then 2013, and had passionately believed that it would do the district well. She had trusted the cause, followed the leadership and the dream of all the good the freedom to govern themselves would bring them. But, turns out, while she did that, the leaders were busy cutting deals for themselves. This time, as much as she believed the cause, she was mistrusting of the leader's intentions, she thought they'd just prolong it for their own gains.'

'That's stuff you say.'

'Hmm.'

'But you know it could be a trap, Ina. I really hope you didn't say anything to her.'

'No, we only listened. She said it took her two agitations to spot the pattern. She felt like the leaders of neither side really cared about the people, and it only took a few meetings and a decent offer for them to forget all the hard work of the people that had gone into fighting for the cause, a cause she had put her life and the life of her family on hold for.'

'What do you mean?'

'She lost her son at the time of the second agitation. He'd been sick. And she hadn't paid enough attention to him. She'd dreamed of working to bring better medical care once they won. But well ... Her husband left her soon after because he blamed her for it. She blames herself still.'

'Oh ... umm ... that sucks.'

'Yes, well.'

'Ina, honestly, I don't know what I think about any of this still, but I am sorry I never listened to you before.'

'But Pem, I never cared that you didn't listen. I just want you to make a choice for yourself, an informed one.'

'Ya ...'

'Anyway.'

'So what happened then?'

'Well, we made a run for it as soon as we could breathe again, and we got back all right.'

'Hmm.'

'Though I don't understand how the goons got there.'

'I guess because they're like goons or something? I mean, they looked violent as hell with their torches and stuff. I swear I was shitting my pants until I got home.'

'I suppose. I wonder what happened with the family. I really hope they are safe.'

'I'm super glad *you* are safe.'

'And I'm glad you are, Pem. We were so worried. But if the family were discovered, they could ...'

'I'm sure they are fine. Uncle had gone in before the men got close to the bungalow. And the whole thing with us must have totally distracted them. Did you see how many followed you?'

'Two.'

'There were three, right? And I know one followed me. So the family is safe.'

'What if the men went back for them?'

'No, I'm pretty sure they didn't. Do you really think they would have run after us when they could have looked for what was right in front of them if they knew?'

'You're right.'

'I'll try go see tomorrow, okay?'

'No no, that might be dangerous.'

'I'll try.'

'Hey, Pem.'

'Ya?'

'You said ... does this mean, you know, what do you make of everything that's happening now? This agitation and promises?'

'I don't know, Ina. I don't know enough to say if all this won't be good for us or something. I think, if it happened, it could actually be good for the town and its people and stuff. But I guess this isn't the way to make it happen, plus I don't know if it will happen at all and what the right way is.'

'Hmm.'

'But like honestly, I have no idea what is actually good at this point.'

'Wait. I think Nidra is hooting. She said she would if Miss Ruth was back.'

'Cool cool, you go. We'll chat soon?'

'Yes, the next time Miss Ruth goes out for a long romantic chat, which shouldn't take long.'

I laughed. Although I felt sick as fuck. I kind of knew I wouldn't see Ina anytime soon, not until the school reopened, definitely not after all this crazy chaos and pretty much all of us realizing that we had been insanely stupid to do this, twice.

'See you soon,' I typed.

'Hey, Pem.'

'Ya?'

'I'm sorry.'

'What for?'

'If it wasn't for me, both Nidra and you wouldn't have gone through this.'

'Ina, what you wanted to do was super nice. And I wanted to come with you.'

'Hmm. I'm still sorry. And I'm proud of you for wanting to think about all this for yourself.'

I smiled.

'Anyway, see you soon, and keep writing!' and she was offline.

CHAPTER 19

NIDRA

I swear, scared just does not describe how I felt last night. I have never had an out-of-body experience, but it felt like ... like Chloë Moretz in *If I Stay* after the car accident. How her body was in coma but her spirit wandered around, dealing with the chaos all around her. Yesterday, while Ina and I ran like headless chickens for our lives, it felt like it wasn't me running at all, as if it was Inayat with some third person while I watched from above or something.

Chloë ... I remember dancing for Mummy while Cholë played her cello on the TV in the background. It was super cool, if I may say so myself, and Mummy had loved it too. She'd told me she was so proud of me. For a while now I have dreamed of being part of an opera, imagine an opera with Indian classical singing. Although when I'd first danced to the cello, I dreamed of this solo performance to the music with Emma Watson reading something from her favourite book. I've been obsessed with Emma for a long time, especially after I saw *Perks of Being a Wallflower*—thoughtful, loving, fun, honest, sort of free and ridiculously kind—we all need a Sam in our lives.

Now that I think about it, Ina kinda reminds me of Sam. Maybe it's the short hair and the side-swept bangs. Maybe it's her brown eyes that have this weird look, as if she knows exactly what's going on, and that smile that almost knows the right thing to say next. Or maybe it's the way she talks, super chill but also ... oh there was a really cool word that Miss Lama used the other day … of course she meant it as an insult but … sagacious! That's it, she speaks sagaciously.

Good thing I said 'felt' huh. Because clearly I have recovered from the shock of last evening with all these daydreams.

Inayat said it could be 'the relief of having come out from it alive'. Perhaps we're hallucinating, I said, and we laughed. 'Or maybe you're trying to brush this under the carpet too!' she taunted. She was right. It was the first time since we heard about the agitation that I had had to confront it, and like this, I mean, this aggressively. All this while I was pretty happy to live in my bubble. And now, even after being hit by reality, I just wanted to get back to it, feel safe there. But I knew Ina wanted to talk.

The two of us sat in the common room with our last mug of watered-down hot chocolate and Parle-G instead of going down to the garden. I think we both needed a break from the general area and the flashbacks of running back up the hill and through the graveyard before finally falling down on the ground for a breath.

'What happened last night …' she said, switching on the heater and moving it towards us. 'Have you made sense of it?'

I shrugged.

'I haven't, even after all the writing I did. It feels Dalí surreal.'

'But I guess it might be best to simply … well … forget.'

'But, Nidra. Could we really?'

'I dunno. I know I haven't felt this unsafe ever before. I have never thought of the outside world as this unsafe before. It made me realize that it's … *bad* … out there.'

'I know what you mean. We never think about it I guess, but all the times we read about politics and war, the thought of who really is bearing the brunt of it and who is reaping the benefits isn't given a second thought.'

'Until it happens to us I guess …'

'I worry about what happened to the family, you know,' Inayat sighed.

'I am sure they are fine. We know the men ran after the three of us. And it was a super nice thing you wanted to do for them.'

'Nidra, I am sorry I put you through this. It was very dangerous, and I should have thought it through.'

'Ina, honestly you've gotta …'

'I know what you are going to say, Pema said the same, but I still had to tell you that I didn't mean to put either of you in harm's way.' I pulled myself closer to her and took her hand in mine, the knots, the butterflies I had gotten used to having around Ina growing in my stomach. 'We're in a safe place now, right?'

'You know, it does feel like home here now.'

'I told you!' I jumped, grabbing her by her shoulders.

'I know, I know. I guess, as the old lady said, it takes a lot of courage to see through our own biases and admit the truth?'

I laughed. 'I cannot believe I am hearing Inayat praise herself!'

'I'm not. I'm just saying …'

'I know what you're saying Inayat Zia!' I said, laughing excitedly.

'Hey, don't spill the hot choco.'

'You mean hot chocolate slush.'

'Something's better than nothing. At least Wai Wai like it,' Inayat said, stroking one of the two house cats, Wai and Wai, who got busy licking the spilled drink.

'You know … speaking of admissions … I gotta say, as much as I have hated my mother not coming early and having to stay in school for so long, I think I have enjoyed my time here in the last few weeks.'

'My turn to say I told you so?'

'Well, you didn't really say it, did you?'

She chuckled. 'I guess not.'

'But I know you made me feel that way. And actions over words, no? I mean, how many times has my mother said something and not followed through? In fact, we all talk about this all the time. How often do our parents say they love us but show us otherwise in a gazillion ways? Like Nitisha's parents, who have forced her to take commerce despite her wanting to pursue humanities because *they* think it will be lucrative. Riya is yelled at so often, so brutally, and is so scared of making a mistake that she actually gets a panic attack every time she so much as drops something and hears anyone walk up; and she feels this here too, far away from home! It's crazy. I mean, Avantika's parents have criticized everything she does so much that she never feels like she is doing enough. She is always afraid of doing anything different from what her family plans for her and being anything but the best. And Ignaz's mother has endlessly punished Ignaz for having a boyfriend when she herself has one who her father knows nothing about. Does any of it really show love? Did it really show love when my mother chose to travel the world and win accolades rather than be home with me, even when that gardener felt me up to put it lightly, or when I told her I was unhappy being alone?' I stopped for a breath. 'Sorry, I didn't mean to go on a rant or whatever. I was really actually only trying to say thank you.'

'No, don't be ...' Inayat turned to look at me, her hand letting go of mine to pull me in by my waist. I could feel her breath on my face as she leaned in, and I felt my heartbeat quicken, ready to beat right out of my chest as she stroked my cheek with her fingers and then my lips.

'Dinner, girls!' Miss Ruth's voice interrupted.

We got up quickly and rushed out, our faces flushed in anticipation of what could have happened.

'We'll talk about this, I promise,' Inayat said, squeezing my hand one final time. 'I heard you, and there is something I want to share with you too. Maybe we could talk about this at length later, take our last Indomie to the graveyard?'

I nodded.

CHAPTER 20

INAYAT

God,
    We kissed.
    My stomach is still in knots, and I can't get my heart to stop racing enough to talk to you about how it all happened, but I'll try.
    We kissed. We kissed!
    And for all the kisses I've seen in movies and read and reread about in books, this was, let's just say they all fell short of how surreal this was. It was plucked from in between the pages of my favourite novels and yet nothing like any of it.
    You know, I have never been someone who spent endless hours thinking about what my first kiss might be like, or for that matter who it might be with. And I feel so grateful for it, because perhaps that is why this felt the way it did, as easy as it did, and comfortable, even though my heart felt like it would burst out of my chest at any minute.
    I can't tell if I did it right. I tried to remember what Rainbow Rowell wrote about Cath and Levi's kiss, what Veronica Rossi said about Aria and Perry's, what I'd seen of Harry and Ginny's first and the many many more I ought to have remembered, but it all came to me in jumbled nothings, like my brain had stopped working altogether as soon as she leaned in and held my face in her hands.
    So I gave up and closed my eyes, my lips parting as they touched hers, quivering shyly against her confident ones.

I have always thought I only lived fully, no thoughts of the past or future, when I am on the wheel, but in that moment, I don't remember anything but us. I don't remember if it was cold, if the wind blew, or if we heard distant noises from the school and town. In fact, I think details from earlier in the evening slipped away too. All that agony I had been feeling about everything we had witnessed in the last few days melted away.

All I remember is how her lips felt against mine, how softly ours touched, opening ever so slightly before they came together to become one again, how her breath felt on my face, electric and yet calming in some way. I can still feel her hands as they moved from my face to my back, pulling me closer. When her tongue felt the shape of my mouth, parting my lips to feel my moist insides, I don't think I can yet put into words what it did to me, but I knew it wasn't just my heart and mind that felt it. As she slid her arm under my skirt, her cold against the heat of mine, lifting my legs to sit on hers, I could feel myself tighten, and my, I don't think there is another way of saying vagina, well, my nethersphere, throb up to my stomach that was in knots.

I was happy before it too.

We had gone down to the graveyard at night and were picking up where we had left off before Miss Ruth called us for dinner—about our mothers yet again.

Nidra was telling me about hers. She had a beautiful, happy childhood, something we had in common. Her parents were in love, and they travelled the country with her father's army job. Every posting was a new adventure. Until a diffusion gone wrong left the mother-daughter on their own.

'Mummy made sure we were happy even after. We made a home for the two of us and she made sure I didn't miss Dad,' Nidra said. 'But it all changed when she got busier with her jobs. She missed so much of my life, and I was alone very often. It was crazy lonely.'

'I suppose she was lonely too, and work made her, well, less alone?' I reasoned, but she didn't hear me.

'And when I told her about the gardener, she told me it was my fault that I went to him and decided to send me off to St Mary's.

We never spoke about it after. Which was different to begin with. We always spoke of everything. And, I've kind of always felt alone ever since. Maybe she felt angry, or guilty, like she was to blame for not being around, and I've blamed her too honestly, but only because I wish she would have spoken to me instead of letting the doctor do the work, because her distance made me lose my best friend in her. I wish she'd asked me how I was, what I needed. I wanted to hug her, cry, tell her how it happened. I felt so insanely lost. Over the years I have forgotten so much, it was easiest to really, and I have worked hard to rebuild what I have and am today on my own.'

I reached out to hold her hand in mine, to let her know I was there for her. Sometimes there isn't much we can say to change how the other person feels but we can do everything to make them feel like they are not alone in it. 'It wasn't you, Nidra. You were a child. You didn't know.'

Her distant look told me she was listening to what I had to say but was not receptive to it.

'I guess I know a little something about how life can change so quickly,' I said, changing the subject.

She turned to look at me.

I told her of my time growing up in Delhi, and all the fun Ammi, Abba and I had when Abba wasn't travelling. How there was never a night when Abba was at home and we didn't play board games or watch a movie or cook together. How we always found a way to have fun. I told her about Arshia and how every night I prayed to say thank you for the life I had. I needed nothing else.

Of course, all of that brought me to when the fun ended—when Ammi found out that every time Abba was travelling he was only travelling to another bed in the same city—and how it was never the same ever again.

'I guess she is happy now, no?' Nidra asked.

'Yes, without me.'

It was her turn to squeeze my hand.

In that moment, in a way I had never felt with anyone before, I felt understood. And she didn't say it out loud, but I knew she felt the same. Because when she turned around to look at me, her eyes rested on my face with the same serenity that I knew I had in mine.

That is when it happened, when she leaned in, held my hair between her fingers and kissed me.

I don't know for how long we kissed, but when we stopped to look at each other, my happiness had been replaced by something greater, something more like exhilaration, clouded with guilt.

I don't know if I can make sense of what happened, or if I want to. I've read queer love stories, and they read just like any other love story. Perhaps because they are all just people in love really, what's the difference, right? But I've also often heard how 'unnatural' it is for boys to kiss one another, or girls each other. How it is unacceptable to you. But, it didn't feel wrong to me, not until my mind piped in. Do you think what I have done, what I am feeling is haram? Ought I to respond to this feeling of guilt? Am I going against everything Nani Nana have taught me? How can it be wrong for two people who care for each other to show it and share it with one another? Can love that doesn't cause harm to anyone be wrong?

Yes, I said love. I know I feel it. I know I've seen it build ever since I met Nidra in the graveyard the first week in school and felt better with her like I only have with Nani. And I could tell it was love that day by the lake. I am always calmer around her, my unhindered self. She's brought back joy in my life, the joy I had known long ago with Ammi Abba and then for a brief while with Nani Nana and Sidra Di. I just don't think I stopped to make sense of it until tonight. And I have now. It's like John Green said, 'I fell in love the way you fall asleep: slowly, and then all at once.' But I am struggling to understand if what I'm feeling for Nidra is wrong, if what we've done is condemned by you, if you think I am going against everything you have decreed of us. I am going to pray the istikhara tonight, knowing you will show me the way, knowing that whatever comes to me then will be your will.

Yours, Ina

CHAPTER 21

NIDRA

This is crazy strange.

I remember my first kiss. It was Rohan. He was a dancer too. I was back home for the holidays and he was in my salsa class. We became dance partners and then friends in only a few days. He was funny, lots of fun, and we hung out every day that winter, even days when he was meant to be at school.

Some days he took me to places I had never heard of in Delhi. On other nights we sneaked out to the water tank in the colony and sat for hours. We had very similar dreams, and it was pretty cool to share them with him.

It was on one of those nights, on the tank. There was no great romantic moment as such. We were just talking about random things, he was flirting and I remember blushing, and he held me by the waist and pulled me in and kissed me lightly first. I didn't know what to do with my hands, so I kept them stuck on the floor by my side. I didn't know how to move my mouth, so I just let him do the kissing.

The next few days we kissed some more and it got better. It was slimy sometimes (when he tried to get his tongue inside my mouth and swirl it around which was kinda icky), perfect a few others (when he kissed me gently, slowly, holding me close), even weird once (when he put his hands under my t-shirt and I slapped it off. There is something about touching breasts; even if I ever do it to myself, it makes me sad and uncomfortable. Thankfully, he never tried again). It was one of the best holidays I told him, and I meant it then. I was very happy.

When I was leaving he asked me if I wanted to be his girlfriend. I said yes and we kissed again. We promised to write. And I did, against my hatred for it, against all matron's inspections before posting. I wrote every week, telling him about school and how I couldn't wait to see him and the stuff we could do when we were together. He wrote back thrice, the last time to tell me that he didn't think it was working out, that he had met someone he liked and since she was in the same city it was just easier. Whatever. I didn't write back and went to a different dance class once I got back for the holidays.

I had met other boys since, kissed many more and gotten the hang of it, even been to third base with one, my last, Sid. But *this* just felt strange. Maybe because it was with a girl. Maybe because it's Ina.

I have really started to like her. I actually love everything about her, trust her, care about her. I am more myself with her that I have been with my friends in all these years, even Mum of late. But couldn't we have just been friends for all that? I don't know. But I know she liked it too though, the way I felt her body let go when we kissed, shivering when our bare thighs touched as I pulled her legs onto mine, her heart racing when I let my hands brush her breasts lightly. I know that happened to me with Sid.

This is just annoying. I don't think I have ever thought about anything as much as this.

Maybe it's also strange because it was a pretty great kiss, with a girl.

'Nidra!' Miss Ruth shouted, barging into the dorm.

'Huh?'

'Don't sit there looking dazed. I have been screaming for you for the last ten minutes. Come down, your mother's going to call again.'

'Oh, sorry. Yes, Miss.'

I climbed out of my bed and into my shoes.

On the call, Mummy was pretty excited.

'I'm on my way, Nidu. I'll be back in Delhi tomorrow and am coming to get you.'

I know I'd wanted Mum to come all this while, and I had sulked about it a hell of a lot, but why wasn't I excited now?

'Nidra?'

'Umm ... yes yes. I'm here.'

'Aren't you excited, darling? I know you're angry with me because I couldn't come sooner, but you know how it is with work. But I *am* coming tomorrow and I'm not going anywhere until your school reopens. We'll have lots of time together.'

'Okay,' I mumbled and put down the phone.

And it struck me, all this time I hadn't thought about Mummy and what she would make of Ina and me at all. She hadn't known of my boyfriends except one. I never felt the need to tell her and she didn't care to find out. But this made me think. What would she think of me? What would she do if she found out? Disown me? What would it mean for our relationship?

What about the girls in school? I remember my friends making fun of the 'lesbian ones'. I had sat with them when they did it, listening to them gossip about girls who were getting 'naughty' under the sheets and whatnot. And I never protested. I'm not strong like that, even though it bothers me that they make fun like this. I mean, I've even laughed with them sometimes.

I can't believe it. I guess I am one of them now, one of the 'lesbian ones'. Does one kiss make you one? But, do I really want it to be only one kiss? Do I still like boys? Am I maybe bisexual? I mean, the idea of boys doesn't disgust me or anything. I think, if I had to be honest, I could still masturbate to Sid and me making out in his room. But all I can think of now is being with Ina again, holding her, kissing her. Oh god, I really don't get what I am feeling at all. Why have I become like this? What am I even?

No, no one can know. I just have to make sure no one finds out. And it'll be fine. As far as everyone knows, Ina and I are friends, and I'm gonna keep it like that. And Ina and I can be whoever we want when we are on our own. Yup, that would be best.

Back in the common room, Ina was reading, of course, Wai snoozing on her lap.

'Hey,' she smiled as I walked in. We hadn't met each other since last night.

I smiled back, kinda awkward. Not because of the kiss I think, although I didn't want to speak about that either, but mostly because speaking meant talking about me leaving tomorrow. But I guess I had to.

'Mummy just called,' I said.

'Oh, and?'

'She's coming tomorrow.'

'That's ... that's great, right?'

'Ya ... I suppose.' I sat down by her. 'You finished reading *Lolita*?'

'Yes, and I issued it in your name so you can read it too.'

I smiled.

'You can take it with you.'

'I will,' I promised.

We sat silently for some time. Not the usual kinds we had. We had a lot of those and they never felt hard or anything. In fact, they were actually decent. But this time it felt hard, like we both had lots to say but just couldn't. Maybe it was because of all the things we were suddenly feeling, anyways Ina feels things a hundred times more intensely than I do.

So I broke it. 'I don't want to go.'

'I wish you could stay,' she said, taking my hand.

And instantly I felt better.

'But I suppose we knew we'd have to leave eventually.'

'Only for some time though,' I comforted us.

'Yes, for some time.'

'Have you heard from your mum?'

'Not yet.'

'I'm sure she will come soon.'

'I'm okay if she doesn't too. I'm happy here. I would rather not go to Amir and her.'

I squeezed her hand a little tighter, and she stroked mine gently with her fingers, sending my heart racing.

'I'm going to miss you.'

'I am too. Let's write to each other?'

'I've seen you write; I'll never catch up. But I promise I will try, unlike Rohan.'

'Rohan?'

I waved my hand. 'Ignore. I'll tell you about my unfortunate first boyfriend some other time. And ya, I promise I'll try writing.'

She smiled.

'I'll see you soon, and then we'll have plenty more hot chocolate for our time with Sister Mary.'

'Nidra!'

'What?'

'I think a date without Sister Mary might be nice, don't you?'

I smiled, taking a moment to digest that she said date. 'Okay, just us and hot chocolate. How about that?'

'And Pema's mummy's chebureki.'

'Oh yes! And some Wai Wai might be nice too.'

'You're going to put the dalda in it though.'

'Of course, I am. It's all the taste!'

CHAPTER 22

INAYAT

Dear Nidra,

You've been gone two days and there is so much to tell you already. But before I begin, I have to ask you to forgive my bad handwriting. I really hope you understand it. It's never great, but it's worse today because I'm on the airplane, and I'm still jittery from the ride down.

Yes, I'm going back home, not to Lucknow with Ammi as I had been dreading, but to Hyderabad with Nani Nana like I'd been praying for. Of course, you already know what I mean when I say home.

Nana was a little better over the last week and insisted that Nani and he come pick me up. They didn't call, just showed up. Nani said Nana was very angry that I wasn't home already in the midst of all of this. I couldn't thank God enough that they came. The school had gotten very lonely since you left, despite all the time I spent in the library and on the pottery wheel (I finally managed to make a Tina Vlassopulos vase without it cracking. Now to pray it stays like that until school reopens so I can fire it).

Anyway, I don't think I've told you this, but Nana was a doctor in the army and he thought it might be easier for him to get through in the bandh with some assistance. Honestly, it wasn't. In fact, if anything, it turned out to be more difficult.

With the army personnel in the car with us, we were stopped every fifteen minutes of the three-hour drive for a check by men who were definitely not from the police—they reminded me of the men at the house that night—and every time I held onto Nani and Nana like I was holding on for my life, convinced of the worst. Nani says that we are often destined for something but we alter it with our actions and duas. I know it's going to sound weird, but I couldn't help thinking I was destined to die, ever since that night we sneaked out, and the destiny was still holding onto me somehow.

The driver and the army personnel with us were harangued too many times to count, even jostled on a few occasions. At one stop post they pointed a gun at the army officer and threatened to kill him, set an example of their determination and cause, they said. The army personnel didn't try to dispel the danger either. And I don't know who gives the orders and what they are, but from where I sat it felt like a real example of an eye for an eye honestly. I don't think I can ever get rid of the memory of those minutes. The guns that we've all seen strapped up out this time and pointing at living people. For the first time I thought about how powerful, how dangerous something as small could be. It wasn't on me and yet I saw all our lives, and—I hate to talk in idioms, but there is no other way to describe this than—flash before my eyes.

Not a peep came out of any of us. We just sat huddled in the backseat, Nani holding onto both Nana and me. 'Not anymore,' she sobbed to Nana when he wanted to go out to sort it. And for the first time I realized what her life might have been like all those years travelling with him in the army. Now that I think about it, in all time months of staying with her, she never spoke about her life, and I never asked her about it either. How selfish and self-centred I must be to think of nothing but my own plight. Perhaps that is what God is trying to teach me from all this. Perhaps this is the indication I need to turn outward instead.

And luckily, I get the chance to do that. Because if it hadn't been for a man who came out of the post and whispered something into the other's ears, immediately making him lower his gun, I cannot imagine what might have happened.

I keep thanking God for protecting us. I sobbed as I thanked the driver when we finally reached the airport, who despite it all promised to get us to the airport safely.

'We're all brothers in arms, naani,' he said, 'and I don't mean just on the battlefield.'

I'm still trying to decipher the second part of it. You must tell me if you understand.

I think all three of us heaved a sigh of relief only when the flight took off. Nani and Nana slept off immediately, still are. I'm sure this must have tired them immensely, and I feel guilty that they had to go through this for me when Ammi could have been here, but I am very grateful to them. And I wanted nothing more than to write to you. God might be angry with me, because this might have been the time that I journal to him, but he brought me to you, so I'm sure it's all part of his plan and he'll understand. Meanwhile, I am trying to make sense of all these feelings myself.

But look at me. I just wrote pages about everything that has happened to me and have not asked how you are and what you are doing. Another reminder of me being self-centred. I'm sorry. I hope your time back with your mother is everything you have talked about, all the memories you have with her and the plans you had for when you would spend time again.

My address will be on the envelope, and Nani Nana's landline number if you ever want to call. I hope to hear from you soon.

Yours, Ina

P.S. I miss you. So much.

P.P.S. I will email you soon. I know that will be a hundred times faster, but you know how I feel about reading things on paper, and I had to make sure our first letter was handwritten.

CHAPTER 23

PEMA

No one has written a letter to me before, like ever! When Dada moved to college, I wrote to him a few times, and he literally just sent back some stupid signed cards and imli sweets he got on the airplane, which apparently he loved and was totally sacrificing for me. What crap. And of course I've never got a love letter like so many girls in school (ya ya, I know I sound like bitter, but come on, I mean, do I even have to explain), or even those little chits that are passed between boys and girls during school events and outings. You know, apart from all the gazillion downsides of being in St Mary's I've mentioned before, I think, just maybe, if I was in regular school, I might have met more boys from town and then maybe one would have liked me, because they also look like me, and then I might have had a boyfriend.

But anyways, I was saying ... this was like a real letter. From my best friend. Well, almost. It was an email, but this was the second-best thing to a real letter since the post office was closed anyways. And it was a damn long one too, not that I doubted that Ina could write this much.

I hadn't spoken to Ina since that night at the chowr. I had left her a few DMs, but with all the cell towers in town being cut off in the bandh, the only way I could check my email was if I managed to force myself to sneak out with Baba's phone to this one spot in the Mall Road where you could catch the signal from Sikkim. And honestly, that night out had completely freaked me out. I hated even going out to the garden. Initially Aama was worried about me, and then she just got mad. She even beat me up when I said I wouldn't go out to pick the clothes when it started raining this one time after the incident. I mean, she hasn't hit me in years, but that day she hit me like old times. And then she beat me more when I (and I totally made sense let me tell you) told her that beating me was only delaying picking the clothes and getting them more wet, which is never good in Darj, where nothing dries up anyways. I mean, I think it was more about her shop being burnt down in one of the recent 'skirmishes' between the army and local party members in town. But I'll talk about that in a bit. First the letter.

With no other way to do this, I had to somehow gather all the courage to sneak out to send Ina another DM, and that's when I got it, right on top of my inbox. She said she had just got to her Nani Nana's in Hyderabad and had a lot to tell me. I mean, I knew Ina could write, I had seen her write in her diary when I'd slept over at school, but the length of her email got me really excited. I wanted to read it like immediately then, but I knew Aama would call me for lunch soon and didn't want to deal with her anger again if she found out I wasn't home. Plus Baba being away for party meetings only meant that Aama would already be boiling. So I decided I'd make like my own sleepover party of it.

I got done with lunch, sneaked in a packet of Wai Wai (because there was no way I could cook Maggi under Aama's nose) and snuggled in with Errol to read. I hadn't been this excited in days.

She said that she'd missed me ... *yayyyy* ... that more girls had left since the last time we spoke and the school was almost empty by the time she left. She apologized some more about that night ... *psycho she is* ... and asked me to thank Aama for the snacks, they had really helped in the last few weeks.

I mixed the dalda in the Wai Wai and gave it a good shake before adding the masala (that's the only way to make sure that the masala sticks to the Wai Wai properly). I took a last lick of the masala packet and let Errol do the same. Errol loves Wai Wai, same as Ina. Maybe when things reopen I could ask Baba to find a way to become Ina's local guardian, and then she could take outings and we could have sleepovers at home, like all my cousins and neighbours do with their friends. We would have Wai Wai and Maggi, watch *13 Reasons Why* (I still haven't watched it and everyone in school has been talking about how great it is) and *The Bold Type*, even have a bonfire and roast those marshmallows Mummy saves for my birthday.

Oh god, I missed her more than I already was and prayed that things got back to normal soon so we could start school again. You know, I think hanging out with Ina is making me pray more or something.

I took a handful of the Wai Wai and read on.

She wrote about Nidra. *Ugh, Nidra.* I guess I really have to like accept that they are friends and all. I will just have to make sure that she and I are better ones.

She spoke about how Nidra and she had become like close, how she had helped her settle down in school—*what the fuck, hadn't I helped?*—how Nidra had helped her be less lonely in the evenings after I left—*yes, the boarding vs day scholar thing again, will I ever have an actual best friend?*—and how they had grown closer since the bandh—*just what I feared.*

But why was she telling me all this? I mean, did I really have to know that my best friend had a new best friend and that they spent hours sitting and talking in the graveyard or whatever? Like, what nonsense. I am still trying to get Ina to talk to me like properly and she's telling me how she felt like she could share her worries … *what in my Boju's name does that even mean* … with Nidra, how she told her all about her family and her coming to St Mary's and stuff. Why should I care if Nidra and Ina share things in common, and things brought them together and blah blah blah. What-fucking-ever.

There it goes—another best friend lost, I thought.

She had something important to tell me, she said.

I don't know how to tell you this, Pem. I have thought a lot about how I would tell you, how I would tell everyone actually. It's consumed me for days, thinking about what it all means. I think I know now, but it worries me.

Okay then. She sounded weird.

For some time I even thought I would keep this a secret, it seemed safer that way, but I feel ready to share it with someone, and I don't think I can with anyone else yet. And you, you've become such an important part of my life, such a close friend, well, I want you to be the person I tell.

Okay, happy again. She wants to tell me something no one knows and I'm an important part of her life. I read on.

But I'm scared, Pem. I don't know what you'll think about me after, and I fear it, the social implications. But I feel like you of all people will understand. I hope you do. So here it goes.

Fuck, she needed to get to the point! I could no longer take the suspense. So, I skipped a few lines.

Wait, what! My mind was like going totally nuts. I was so shocked that my hand let go of the Wai Wai packet and Errol quickly put his face into it.

'Errol, stop,' I scolded, and put the packet away on the desk.

Ina was a ... was a lesbian?

I have thought about my sexuality a lot over the last few months. I even Googled it to understand what I was thinking and feeling meant, took a few quizzes and felt stupid about taking them, but I'm pretty convinced that I'm a lesbian.

I like girls. And I like one in particular.

'WHO!' I screamed out loud. 'A book, Aama, got excited about a book,' I yelled out to Aama before she asked. I read again.

Nidra.

What the actual fuck! My head was like bursting at this point. She told me about how she had fallen in love with Nidra, how she felt around her and whatnot, how for so long she couldn't understand what she was feeling but finally got it now, and how they ...

Wait, what again!

They kissed!?

I have read about like girls kissing girls, and boys kissing boys. Every now and then there are rumours in school about girls who were dating each other, but they usually die down in a few weeks without any proof. And I've *seen Orange is the New Black* and only just finished reading *Call Me by Your Name*. And I remember Dada talking about the march that happened across the country for the rights of the queer people and everything, how he thought it was like crazy not to let them have a normal life. Aama was not happy with Dada though. She said it was not normal and stuff, that boys were supposed to like girls and the other way around, that it is how nature wanted it and anything else was abnormal or something. She said it was ridiculous that there were people who could think they were not the gender they were born with. How can a boy randomly say he is a girl, she had asked. They'd fought for hours. I don't remember how it all ended, but they never spoke about it after. I guess bhai decided it would be a never-ending fight, and I didn't bother thinking about it either. I guess, when something's not happening to you directly you can be selfish and not care, no?

But now the letter made me like think. Could *I* kiss a girl? I've always dreamed of my first kiss. It would be with a boy from St Stephen's. He would be handsome, love books and food and swimming and insects. We would meet at a school fest—I'd be sitting, watching the performances, he'd be sitting on a bench in front, and he would turn around and smile and I'd like smile back. He would write me a chit. I would reply. He would laugh and write back, asking me to meet him near the washroom. After a while we would both get up to go, and at the washroom we would talk shyly and exchange emails and numbers. Back home, we'd start talking and plan to meet for a walk. We'd go down Lover's Road and sit to watch the sunset over the Kanchenjunga, and there he would tell me how beautiful I am, hold my hand, ask me to be his girlfriend. And when he'd drop me home, he would say goodbye and bend down to give me a kiss.

What would it be like to kiss a girl? I tried to picture Ina and Nidra kissing in the graveyard but quickly stopped myself. It was weird, and it hurt too too too much to think that Ina had someone who was more special to her than me.

Were Nidra and Ina girlfriend and girlfriend? She didn't say. Nidra had to leave right after, and so did Ina.

Wonder what it'll be like once school reopens? You are definitely not going to be the person she chills with now. My mind added fuel.

Things will change. Ina will want to spend all her time with Nidra, and you will have to go back to having no friends at all. It will be like it's been with all the other girls at school.

I thought about my own sexuality. I wondered why Ina didn't want to date me? Did I want to date her? I mean, I don't know, I had never felt it or even thought about it, but I might have liked to be considered at least now that I knew Ina likes girls.

I wondered what it would be like to date Ina. It might be nice actually. We would spend all the time we had in school together, and then after she could sneak out and come meet me in town, or I could sneak in. But I wasn't sure that meant like you were dating someone. We did that now too. Even then, it would be nice to have someone be *my* person all the time.

But I guess that will not be Ina now.

I stared at the email. I wondered what I felt about her being a lesbian, not my friend but a lesbian, and I realized I didn't think much. I didn't really care if she was a lesbian. I know a lot of girls in school made fun of them and I always went along, but personally I found it stupid, like you can't really choose who you like, no? I didn't think it abnormal or anything, though thinking of Nidra and her together made me … no, I just felt sad honestly. She said she hoped to hear from me soon, but all the excitement I had when I got the email was completely gone. Everything I had to say was taken over by questions, so many questions, plus doubts and crazy fear.

CHAPTER 24

NIDRA

Thank god she told me they were in the airplane right at the get-go, because I couldn't have sat through eight pages (front and back!) of bad handwriting without knowing if they'd reached safely. Eight pages!
　Man, she has horrible handwriting. I'd never noticed.
　Anyway, god, I can't believe what it must have been like for her to have to go through all that harassment. If I knew Ina, she would spend days thinking about it. Unlike me, I kinda forget easily.
　I have to tell her she's wrong. I mean, she isn't self-centred at all. I feel like she overthinks things about herself, a lot, perhaps because of everything that has happened with her. But most of all I hate that she thought she was going to die, or that she could have died, I mean fuck that is insanely dark. I remember the other night the old lady said something about 'innocence being lost' in these political things, and it makes sense now. I had so … what's that word … not wrapped up … but sort of … oh yes, cocooned. I had been so cocooned, at school, in myself, and so much had happened around me. In fact, so much had happened even in the few times I'd stepped out of my bubble that I couldn't ignore it even if I wanted to.
　I thought I'd write her back, I know I'd promised her I'd try, but I really do hate writing, and she had said I could call her, so I picked up the phone instead.
　'Hello? Hello.' I heard the soft voice of a lady on the other end.

'Hello? This is Nidra. Can I speak with Inayat please.'

'Ji, beta. Inayat!'

There was a crackle before I heard Inayat's voice on the other end.

'Hello?'

'Ina!'

'Nidra! Hi! I've been thinking about you, I thought the letter should have reached you by now.'

'I just got it today. Our mailman gives our letters to our neighbours and they forgot to give it to us.'

'Ah.'

'What's up? How are you?'

'I'm okay, and you? Did you read the letter?'

'Of course. Many times. Because it took that long to understand what you'd written,' I laughed.

'I know, I'm sorry.'

'No no. Blame the airplane.'

We laughed.

'Anyway, I am so glad you are back in Hyderabad. I cannot even imagine what happened on the way. I mean, it was difficult even when Mum and I came down, we were checked again and again, but not this bad. Although we passed this building that was burning and that scared her. She was so sorry for not coming sooner.'

'It's nice that she apologized. And yes, we crossed many buildings that had been burnt down, the rail museum in Jorbungalow that Uncle had been talking about, burnt to nothing too.'

'I can't believe what is happening. How do they expect to build the town back up after all this is over. Who would even want to live here?'

'Hmm,' Inayat sighed.

'You know in Harry Potter when Voldemort is coming back to power and the whole world seems dark and joyless or whatever? The drive down was like that. It felt like there was no joy left, like after this is over, whenever that is, all that will be left of it will be burnt broken bits. I feel stupid I never thought about any of this until now.'

'Are you giving me a book reference, Nidra?'

'Are you impressed?' I giggled.

'I am!'

'I was referring to the movie though.'

We laughed and fell silent quickly, just thinking of the situation back in Darjeeling, and because I guess we were both feeling a lot of stuff, about us and god knows everything really, but hadn't spoken about it yet.

'How are Nani Nana and Sidra Di?' I asked, trying to change the topic.

'They're good. They're very happy I'm back. And now that Nana is feeling better, we are back to our usual activities. I've joined pottery class again, and Nani Nana come along sometimes, although they usually sit and do some slab work. Nana enjoys making animals with clay.'

'That's so sweet. I'm so glad you're having fun at home. Will you want to come back to school now?'

'Of course. Ammi's not going to be too happy if I don't. She's coming here with Amir soon.'

'*Now* she comes.'

'Yes.'

'But you'll only come because your mother will force you to?'

I have never been much of a thinker, in fact, I pretty much hate it. It's always been easier to just forget about things, and over the last few days I have tried my hardest not to think about everything I'm feeling about us. There's a lot that I'm feeling. There's too much back and forth in my head about what I want and what I think is the smarter thing to do, considering everything I have seen and everything I want to achieve. But I realized I don't want to make a choice now. And since my plan of not telling anyone should work just fine, I've decided to go with what my heart wants—continuing where Ina and I left off. I think I'm just not ready to let go of her.

'And you,' Inayat whispered. 'I miss you.'

'I miss you too.'

'We never got a chance to talk about that night.'

'We didn't.'

'So?'

'So ...'

'I liked the kiss.'

'I did too.'

'Nidra, I have to be honest about how I feel. I like you. I think I love you actually. I don't know what any of this means, I've never done this before, and I've spent enough time trying to understand if I am a bisexual now, or a lesbian, or whatever I'm feeling means. I'm trying to make sense of what it might mean for my life, and I know I may anger a lot of people in my life, even myself, and there is a chance that some of them may disown me too. I don't have the answers to everything yet, but I know that I don't want to let go of us.'

'Nidra?'

'I like you too.'

'And?'

'And, I don't know.'

'Do you want to date?'

'I don't know what that means, Ina. I've only ever dated guys before, and you …'

'I'm not a guy.'

'Yes. And I don't know what this means.'

'Do we have to know? I know after that night at the lake …'

'I was scared, Ina. I *know* how the girls think about these things, I've seen it. And I promise the nuns do not see this as normal at all. And honestly, I didn't want to feel what I was feeling, so I ran away from you. But I hated it. And then in the bandh being with you was … just super special. I realized that if that's how I feel with you then I didn't want to think about anything else. I didn't want to think even though there is so much going on in my mind about what people would say, what will happen to my life, and with my mum. But then something in my head said we don't have to think about everything right now, we can enjoy what we have. I mean, why mess with something that isn't … that's making us happy? And we don't have to tell everyone about it right now. We can keep it to ourselves.'

'I mean, I suppose so. But …'

'Ina, I don't know what I'm doing here. And I've dated plenty guys before.'

'You have.'

'Are you jealous?' I laughed.

'No no ... no.'

'So, what do you think?'

'Honestly, I know it's hard and it's going to be hard, for a bit at least. I have spent a lot of thought on this. We are told by everyone around us that we are supposed to like boys, in more insidious ways than we can even reckon. And I don't know if you know, but my religion, I am yet to understand the tenets fully myself, but it looks upon this as haram. I am still to make sense of how that changes my understanding of faith and my relationship with god, which is incredibly important to me. But kissing you. Liking you. Wanting to be with you. I know I want you in my life as more than a friend. And who says we can only like one gender? Aren't feelings universal, and genderless? I think we should date. I think I have only started discovering what this feels like and I don't want it to stop. I don't want what we shared in the last few weeks to end.'

'I don't want it to either, Ina.'

'Okay, then we date?'

'We date, yes.'

'Okay.'

'And about not telling anyone, I am not sure about it. I know I would not want to keep this hidden, but if you want to take time on that, I understand.'

'Thank you. I have to go now. Mummy has planned a silly painting class for the two of us and she keeps calling me to hurry.'

'That sounds like fun. Are you having fun being back with her?'

'Lots. I'll tell you more on the next call. I'll drop you an email for when.'

'Okay, see you then.'

'See you. Miss you.'

'I miss you too.'

CHAPTER 25

INAYAT

Dear God,

It's funny how the mind works. For some time now I was convinced that I was at home only in Hyderabad; that Nana, Nani and Sidra Di were the only real family I would ever have. But when we got the email about school reopening, I was excited, honestly excited to be back with Pema and Nidra, back to class, the dorm, the art studio. School feels like home too now. And I am looking forward to spending time in the graveyard, swimming in the lake, sitting endlessly in the library, seeing what has become of my pottery.

Turns out, while I got busy with my life in Hyderabad and dating Nidra, which for now entailed me writing long emails to her and her responding in longer phone calls, things in Darjeeling began to die down, both in my head (for all the anger I showed to Pema on it, I scoffed at myself) and out of it. In only a matter of time there were factions within the party. The local leader was slapped with countless terrorism charges by his close aide before he split (who also claimed the leader was trying to get him killed by the way!), which led the man who had all this while been the face of movement to go into hiding. A perfect opportunity for the state and centre to negotiate with the new leader to end the bandh—peace bought with SOPs and promises of development. Talk about high-stakes drama.

Anyway, as Nani and I packed my bags, it was me assuaging her instead, telling her that I am happy, that school makes me happy and I'll be back home to them in no time. I didn't cry as they dropped me at the airport where I met a few other girls from school. I have found that even forgiving Ammi has become easier.

Of course, it's strange that more than anything I find myself questioning this happiness, this peace. Yet again, it feels as if everything has fallen into place, and I feel like I shouldn't be used to this. I can't seem to understand how we can get so easily used to unhappiness but not the other way around.

At school, it feels as if the last 104 days never happened. We're back to how we left.

Except that everyone came back with a lot of food. Pema's mum made me more snacks and I gave her Nani's special kebabs and homemade chips. And since most of the teachers were in 'back from holiday' mode, we were left to our own accord for the most part of the first few days. So Pema and I were left alone to catch up.

It was a conversation I had been dreading.

In the emails we had exchanged, Pema had said nothing about Nidra, and I hadn't asked either. Perhaps because I was so scared of what she might say. Of course, I hadn't told Nani Nana. There were times that I wanted to, but I wasn't sure what they would make of it and I didn't feel ready to face them just yet. But with Pema, I had told her of everything that had happened, about how I felt, and when she wrote back about everything else but that, I understood that she didn't want to speak about it. And I didn't take it badly either. I suppose it can be a lot to know someone for a while and discover something about them that you had never thought possible. And, the more I thought about it, the more I realized how that was the honest truth, that when we meet people, a boy or a girl, we instinctively think that they like the opposite sex, which shouldn't be the case. I want to believe that Pema was processing her feelings and not saying the first thing that came to her mind, which I was grateful for. Did I feel bad? Yes. Did I think it was better than the negative reaction I was fearing? Absolutely.

What I did feel really bad about was her not asking me how I was doing. As easy as it has been falling for Nidra, it's been hard accepting my own sexuality. I wasn't prepared for it. I hadn't even thought it was a possibility. And Pema was the only one who knew. I couldn't tell Nani Nana forget Ammi until I made sense of it. I might have told Sidra Di but I was afraid she'd tell the others. I've been reading on it, reading on what it all means to you. There are so many opinions, and I wish I had someone to talk to. Despite having Nidra, this whole thing has been exceptionally lonely. Although it doesn't feel like that for her. Nidra seems to have gone back to the usual with her friends and in school. It almost seems like Nidra doesn't want to acknowledge this at all, not to others, not herself, which I guess I expected since she hates having tough conversations, but I had hoped this would be different. But I definitely want to give Pema time. I want some time too—for Nidra and me to be able to just live this; for myself to make sense of the vicious cycle of guilt I have been caught in about what my sexuality means to you and my own faith, and feeling guilty for not feeling guilty when I think of Nidra, and of course what Nani Nana will think of it all.

Amidst all this, I desperately hope for answers from you. If this is wrong, why lead me to it? You make this duniya, and you put in our hearts who we love. You put Nidra in mine. How is it wrong then? Is it wrong?

'So ... umm ... Nidra and you,' Pema said.

'Yes.'

'Are you dating?'

'Yes.'

'I see,' she said.

And then we fell back into our regular chatter of everything that had happened and made plans to ask for permission for a sleepover at her home sometime so we could help rebuild her mother's tea shop.

So much has been destroyed during the last few months. Even though I felt happy about coming back to school, as we drove up, it didn't feel like a town but a battlefield still singeing in the aftermath of a fight over what? Power? Money? Because what happened to the cause?

Thankfully school felt the same old.

After classes, Nidra and I decided to spend time in the graveyard, and as soon as we sat down, I realized how much I had missed her.

'I've missed you too,' she said, taking my hand in hers.

I felt my heartbeat quicken as she leaned in and kissed me, pressing her lips gently against mine, opening them a little, feeling them with her tongue before pulling me close and kissing me harder, with more urgency, like she'd been waiting to do this for too long. I know I had.

I think I was better this time too; I heard her moan as I pushed aside her hair to kiss her neck. This time I had read a lot, watched videos, even practiced when I was back home on the back of my hand and my pillow. More guilt.

'I really missed you,' she whispered again, her breath warm against my face.

I felt my cheeks flush as I smiled back.

We stayed there with Sister Mary for a while longer, sharing details we missed on our calls. Nidra had refused to write, and I didn't mind, so we had spoken every day on call instead.

'Pema asked about us today,' I said. I hadn't told Nidra about my first email to Pema, I wanted to speak with Pema first.

'You told Pema about us?' Nidra asked as we got up to leave.

'I thought we decided we wouldn't, Ina, what the hell.'

'I didn't want to keep how I felt a secret, Nidra. And I had told you when we spoke that I didn't want to be hidden. But I respect you not wanting to tell anyone yet. I am not ready to tell the world, that's true too, but Pema is the closest friend I have. And I felt so heavy all the time, I needed to say it out to someone.'

'You don't understand. The girls in school can be brutal about these things. My own friends are capable of turning this into vicious gossip. It gets horrible with the bullying, you don't know. And I definitely don't feel ready to tell anyone or deal with what will happen after. Are you really sure you trust Pema? I mean, not that we can do anything about it now.'

I knew I did. Pema may not understand what's happening, but she would never do anything that would hurt me, I said.

But I've been thinking about what Nidra said about her friends. Why is it that people find solace in bringing other people down? And why hadn't Nidra spoken up before, even though on so many occasions they had done it in front of us? Why did she still spend time with them? What would I do if Pema reacted the same way? I suppose I understand not feeling ready to tell people; I feel it with my family, the worry and fear, but I would think our friends would understand. After all, we are all exposed to so much more that helps us make better sense of the prejudice and the positives.

Perhaps I'll ask her when we sit together next.

Give me strength.

Yours, Ina

CHAPTER 26

NIDRA

I had it all planned. I'd take Ina for a real date, our way. Ready-to-eat Indomie packets amped up with some peanut butter and chilli oil. Hot chocolate with the tiny marshmallows. As many packets of chicken crackers and tomato chilli popcorns as needed. Some of those Korean sweet buns and Nutella sticks. Hot water bottles, bedsheets, fairy lamps, and Ignaz's tablet which had twenty-four new movies including *Everything, Everything,* which I had been meaning to see since Ina forced me to read the book.

But I couldn't find her anywhere. She's usually in the library during tea break, but Mrs Ojha said she hadn't been in all day. The common room was empty too—of course, it was Maggi day, and no one misses that. And, now that I thought about it, I hadn't seen her all day. We usually bump into each other during meals, but she hadn't been there for lunch either. So I got pretty worried. I guess that's what it's like to be dating, you get worried quickly or something.

And I really must not have been thinking straight, because, for some reason, I decided to ask Miss Farzana.

'Miss, have you seen Inayat?'

Of course she yelled at me. 'Why do you need to know? Don't you have anything better to do?'

I have never understood how teachers expect you to answer such questions. 'Umm.'

'Anyway,' of course they cut you off, 'she is in the infirmary, and you are *not* allowed there.'

'Why is she in the infirmary?'

'Because she felt like it would make for a nice holiday.'

But before I could even respond, she said, 'Why does one go to an infirmary, Nidra? Don't ask stupid questions.'

Don't ask stupid questions, don't ask questions at all if possible, the usual teacher motto. I know a failing cause when I see it, and I knew Miss Tabish would be watching the infirmary like a hawk, so there was no sneaking in. I would have to wait till tomorrow to find a way.

And I did. Pema.

Being in the infirmary at St Mary's didn't excuse you from school work, unless of course you were really dying or something, which meant that schoolwork was brought to you in bed. And so, I caught up with Pema.

I had been avoiding her for a while. Knowing that Ina had told her about us made me feel super weird about it. And I was shit scared honestly. I have seen the girls in school bully each other for a hundred different things, and this one was huge! I just wasn't ready for it. I remember what happened with Ruhi last year so clearly. Some of the girls from our dorm read her diary where apparently she'd said something about having a crush on the head girl and wanting to kiss her. And they bullied her about it so much that it kinda broke her. I'd find her crying for hours in the dorm, skipping meals, staying away through the nights. She got so sick after a few weeks that her parents had to pull her out. And I didn't see the girls feel insanely sad about it or anything. They'd forgotten in a few weeks. Being a part of our group didn't stop all the girls from bullying her, calling her a faggot and whatnot. Even I didn't try to make it stop, only consoled her when we were alone. No, I wasn't sure of anyone, but it was either Pema or waiting until Ina came out, and who knew when that would be.

'Hey, Pema.'

'Oh, hey hi. What's up?'

'Not much. I just wanted to check on Ina. Sorry to jump on you like this, but Miss Tabish won't let me in.'

'Me neither, I only get five minutes to give her the classwork,' Pema said.

'What's wrong with her?'

'She has a viral fever, but she should be fine in a few days.'

'Oh no. Okay. Hmm. Do you think ... I don't know.'

'Ya?'

'Do you think you could give a note to her?'

I could see that she was kinda hesitant, and it made me more unsure.

'Never mind, it's okay, I get it.'

'No no, it's okay,' she said finally.

'Really?'

'Ya, for sure.'

'Babe, thank you so much!' I shouted. 'I'll give it to you tomorrow morning? I'm sorry to do this. I know it's stupid, but you know ...'

'Hmm. It's fine. You can give it to me tomorrow. I will go to her at fruit break.'

'Done. And seriously babe, thank you.'

'See you.'

'And will you tell her that I hope she gets well soon and that I'll write to her today?'

'Sure.'

I quickly ran up to write a chit. Of course Ina found a way to get me to write.

Dearest Ina—how are you? Are you feeling any better? I looked for you all day and got so scared when Miss Farzana told me you were in the infirmary. So I found Pema and asked her to give you this note. She was very sweet and said yes. I hope you get better soon. I cannot believe you've gotten sick as soon as school started. We've had no time together since we got back. Hopefully soon. I have a nice picnic planned once you are back. Love, Nidra. And yes, you got me to write. Send a note with Pema please.

The next day at fruit break I waited near the infirmary and gave Pema the note. 'Thank you, Pema.'

She smiled.

'Oh, wait.' I plucked one of those wild white flowers that grow behind the infirmary, the cute one we played that question game with, and handed it to Pema. 'This too please.'

Later in the day she found me again.

'Hey.'

'Oh hey, Pema. Is everything okay?'

'Ya ya, she's okay. She asked me to give this to you,' she said, handing me a note.

I swear, I have never been this excited about reading ever in my life. So weird.

'Would it be cool if ...'

'Yup,' Pema said, even before I could finish. 'Ina was very happy about your note. I'll see you tomorrow at fruit break.'

I ran to the washroom and opened the piece of paper.

I am sorry I scared you. I was feeling feverish in class and went to Miss Tabish for a medicine. But she ran a few tests and got me admitted instead. Don't worry, I'm really okay. I feel a little weak, but I want to believe it is more the hospital food than anything else. I have had nothing but khichdi and dahi for all my meals, although Pema managed to sneak in a sha phaley for me today. If I liked it earlier, I am certain it just became my favourite food ever. This one had so much cheese! I am keeping up with schoolwork, so that keeps me busy, and the rest of the time I spend reading, although Miss Tabish says I should rest my eyes so I have to read under my quilt sometimes. There is no one else in the infirmary, and it is almost nice to have the place to myself, although it would have been nicer if you were around. I can't wait for us to have time alone. I was so happy to see your note, finally! Keep writing, although I hope I am out of here soon. I'm excited about the picnic.

Back in the dorm, I put away the note under my bed and tore a piece of paper to write again.

CHAPTER 27

PEMA

Ina refuses to tell me what she writes in her notes to Nidra, or what Nidra says in hers. Not that I've actually asked, but she seems like super secretive about them, and it's really pissing me off. Especially because *I'm* the one who's been doing this stupid exchanging notes business for them for four days, and *I'm* the one who has to wait while Ina reads Nidra's notes and writes back. I mean, why should I have to do it? Like, what do I get? Ina and I spend whatever time we have in understanding the schoolwork now that the teachers have suddenly realized there's lots to cover thanks to the three-month lockdown, and she spends the rest reading and replying to the notes while I wait. Plus, honestly, I run the risk of getting caught. And at what cost—losing my best friend to her new girlfriend? I am really beginning to wonder if any of this is like worth it.

All this week I've waited behind the infirmary during fruit break for Nidra to come give me her note, and then again after break to give her Ina's. I mean, sure, she comes on time and stuff, but it's all sneaky AF you know, and I wonder why I'm in the middle of all this.

Of course, it doesn't help that it's the one area that the school gardener just doesn't work on, and it has the classic Darj wild grass and mush combo, which is like beyond yuck as hell and gives me the creeps.

Anyways, Nidra's letter seemed heavier today and I got curious. So, once she left, I did something kind of shady—I opened it. Hey, before you judge me and stuff ... well, okay, you can I guess, I am judging myself too. But I'm hoping you understand my headspace.

Anyways, I was saying, I opened it.

In the envelope was a chilli cheese cube, and some chocolate. And now that I had opened it ... and yes it gets worse ... I quickly read what she'd written.

... Since you mentioned yet another day of bad khichdi at the infirmary, I thought I would send you some of our tuck ...

Our tuck? Now they have shared tuck? I thought only Ina and I shared tuck. Was she sharing Aama's snacks with Nidra too? I was beginning to get pissed as hell. And what about me bringing her food to eat because she was hating the meals at the infirmary? Why did she need more food? Did she not tell her I was getting her food? Was my food not good enough? I was jealous and how.

I read on.

... Come back soon so we can go back to the graveyard for our midnight picnic. I miss you.

Of course, they have all these things to do together after school. After I have gone back home all alone. I swear my mind was going to explode. And I don't know why. It wasn't like I hadn't known any of this. I have a pretty decent imagination, and even if Ina hadn't told me everything, I had managed to catastrophize quite a lot of it on my own. So why was I so triggered? Whatever, I just was. I was like so fuming mad that instead of going to the infirmary I went back to the class, refusing to give the letter to Ina. Nope, I wasn't going to do this anymore.

'Hey, Pem. All okay?' Shefali asked as I walked in.

'Huh?'

'You look weird,' she said.

'Weird?'

'No, just, I don't know.'

'I'm just annoyed as hell.'

'What about?'

Okay, in that moment I should have remembered that although Shef's like a class friend, she's also a massive gossip. She loves loves

loves to poke her nose everywhere and dish out shit on everyone. She spares no one. Plus I knew she was trying everything to become the teacher's pet ever since she set her eyes on the head girl badge. I also should have remembered that I love Ina, and all the things Aama had told me about regulating my emotions. But I guess all that anger I felt just didn't let me think straight. So I kind of massively fucked up—I told her why I was mad.

'They're girlfriends?' she asked.

'Yes, I suppose so. And I am exchanging notes for them because Ina is in the infirmary. But why the fuck should I?'

'You don't have to.'

'I guess.'

'But are you sure they are dating?' she asked.

'I think so.'

'Do you have one of their letters with you? Show me! Show me now Pe—'

And I snapped. Shefali wasn't interested in consoling me, she just wanted the dish.

I realized what I'd done, how badly I had fucked up, and tears started pouring silently down my face.

'Stop it, Shef,' Charu interrupted, rushing to me. 'You've really lost it. Pem are you okay …'

But with a crazy sinking feeling taking over me, I ran out of the class and to the infirmary, the letter clutched tightly to my chest.

Fuck fuck fuck fuck fuck. What the hell had I just done.

I stood at the door of the infirmary, unsure of what I should do. I knew the information about Ina and Nidra dating was like dynamite in Shef's hands. Even with rumours the girls were able to do real damage on their own. With what I had told Shef, god knows what she would do. No, it wasn't just about gossip this time, it was about Shef using it to god knows what end.

Should I tell Ina? Would she ever forgive me? What if I lose her, the only real friend I have ever had?

I tried to calm myself down. Okay, what had I told Shef? I don't think I was clear. I had said I was exchanging notes between them. But there was no proof, right? And I stopped as soon as I started. I could tell Ina to be careful. And she never has to know I said anything. I couldn't afford to lose Ina, no, that can't happen. And I was hoping against hope that Shef would not do real harm since I had been nice to her all these years. Maybe I could tell Shef to not tell anyone, although that might mean I was confirming things.

Yes, saying nothing might be best, for now anyways, I thought.

'Pem!' Ina interrupted my thoughts.

'Oh, hey hi,' I stammered. I didn't know if I had it in me to face her, but losing her was not an option.

'Hey, are you okay? I've been waiting for you,' Ina smiled.

'Oh, I just got delayed, had some work. Here is your letter.'

She opened it up excitedly and laughed.

'More junk!' she exclaimed, showing me the cheese and chocolate.

I tried to smile.

She read the letter quietly and picked up her notepad to write hers. I sat quietly, a hundred times more patiently than I had in the last few days. *The things guilt makes you do,* my mind said.

'We really have to get Uncle to speak about the sleepover so we can paint your mother's shop,' Ina said as she wrote. 'I have been thinking of all the things we could do. How about Mad Hatter's tea party?'

More guilt.

'That would be nice.'

'We'll do it as soon as I'm out. I should be by tomorrow. I told matron today, but she said I'd have to wait for Miss Tabish's evening rounds.'

I stayed shut.

Once she had finished writing, she folded the note and handed it to me. 'I am sorry we keep making you do this. Hopefully it should be the last time. Thank you so much though, I know we are both very grateful. I was just telling Nidra how happy I am to see you every day and how your mother's food has helped sustain me once again.'

I teared up again.

'What's wrong, Pem?' Ina said, reaching for my hand.

I shook my head. 'Nothing. I should go.'

'Are you sure?'
I nodded.
'Okay.'
I ran out of the infirmary and into Nidra.
'Hey, there you are,' Nidra said.
'Hi, sorry. Ya ... umm ... here you go,' I said, shoving the letter into Nidra's hands.

I swear, the rest of the day was ... I don't even know what it was honestly, or what I felt. I've never felt like this. Guilt. Self-hatred. Disgust. Dread. Anger. All of it while I tried hard not to break down and to keep away from Shef. The few times she tried to hound me I told her to shut up, that she had completely lost it and I had no idea what she was talking about. But I knew I made no sense and that she didn't buy any of it, not when my face gave it away. A few other times I was grateful Charu told her to fuck off, but I wasn't sure it helped either. I didn't know if being silent was better, or if I should have told her in confidence and begged her to keep my secret. I didn't know anything at this point. I wanted to puke.

CHAPTER 28

INAYAT

God,

For the first time ever, I feel like I have nothing to say to you anymore, and yet I must be a fool to have found yet another page to fill you in on.

But what do I even tell you when I feel like we aren't really friends anymore, like you let me down, like you never did have my back at all. I don't know who does anymore, but of everyone I trusted you the most. And just when I started feeling some semblance of peace, some sense of faith and meaning to life, you took it all away. I can't seem to understand why. Why do it to me? What have I done to deserve this? How am I harming anyone? What wrong am I doing to have all this happen to me? After all my salahs, after all the nafls that Nani prays for me. Nani says there is nothing greater than prayer, that you are always listening and answering, but are you? I have always believed you are. But if you are, then why this? Is it all because I love a girl? Is that what has made me a sinner in your eyes? Or that she doesn't follow your path? How is it that so many out there who are bad people go unaffected, living their lives like their actions have no consequences while we are tested over and over again?

For all these months I have prayed to you endlessly and hoped you would see the love in us, the good in us. I hoped that THAT would be enough for you to bless us. But I suppose not. I feel like I have finally lost all faith, in you, in the people around me, in myself. Nani might not like it, I know she believes that you test the ones closest to you and I must have tawakkul, I must have sabr, but you know what, I am done. Who knows if that will matter too, maybe she will disown me just like you have for the person I am, the person YOU made me. I didn't choose this, just so you know. I didn't choose to like a girl. You chose this for me, destined it for me. I am done being tested and having to prove myself to you. Sure, I haven't followed all the dictates as they are put down, but I know I have never done anything that would harm anyone or anything, and I have always believed in you. I have always believed in being a good person. And if that isn't enough, then this is it. I don't care anymore.

I mean, you didn't even spare us a little when you made us fall.

I was so excited to meet Nidra once I got out of the infirmary. First the bandh and then my illness, we just hadn't had time together. I wanted nothing more than to spend the night in the graveyard with her. And it was a beautiful night too. The sky was clear, and the grass was dry so we could set our bedsheet and lie down. And Nidra had it all planned with our favourite snacks and a movie to watch. But of course you didn't let us be there too long, did you?

We would have been lying down for what, five minutes perhaps, when we heard the screams of Miss Farzana. I can't remember what she said. It is all such a haze now. I suppose it would be when you are pulled apart by your hair in the middle of a kiss. Oh yes, you didn't leave room for explanations. You just thought, let me not give them any sliver of hope at all to come out of this intact. You didn't just rock the boat, you also set fire to it and danced on the burning deck.

My head is reeling from the walk to Sister Teresa's office, both of us on either side of Miss Farzana while Shefali from my class walked sniggering alongside, my diary and our letters in her hand. I wondered how they had found out, but it didn't take me long to find an answer to that. You do answer somethings I suppose. Yes, Shefali spilled it out loud and clear as she handed the writings to Sister Teresa.

'Pema told me that they were girlfriends, Sister. They were making her pass notes for them. I couldn't let that happen. Some of my friends found these in Inayat's cupboard ...'

Pema ... I still cannot believe it. I don't think I even paid attention to the fact that Shefali had invaded my space, broken into my cupboard to find my letters, why she so desperately wanted to bring us down that she did all this and even got her friends to help. No, I stopped at Pema. So, you didn't just take away my dignity, my girlfriend, but also my best friend. Kudos to you, God.

To think how a day can change everything if you will it. We could wake up feeling protected, loved, healing and happy, and in a few shorts hours you could shatter all those beliefs, just like that.

You know, I really believed in you. I really did. After everything that has happened, after everything I have trusted you with. Maybe if I never wrote to you every day Shefali might not have known enough at all. But I did, and I guess here I am, still writing to you. So the joke is on me. But no, not again. I don't know if I'll ever be able to write again. Not to you, not to anyone else. You have taken that away from me, much like everything else. And perhaps the fault is all mine. I prayed the istikhara, asked you if what I was doing was haram to you. This seems like your answer, your will, but it sure doesn't feel like khayr for me, not like this.

CHAPTER 29

NIDRA

I stood in Sister Teresa's office, paralyzed. It was a room I knew pretty well. I'd been given many outstanding student certificates here. We'd taken our first oath as student body representatives here, vowed to uphold the school's name and be the best leaders and stuff. I knew I had been one, I had been a good student, captain and friend. But I don't think it mattered. I don't think it was about any of the actual rules we had broken either. It was about something that I had no control over at all.

'Hand over your cupboard keys,' Miss Farzana said.

Inayat and I did as we were told, not thinking about the violation of privacy it was, neither arguing that they had been broken into already.

When Miss Farzana and Shefali came back sometime later, they had more letters in their hands. Why had she cared to create so much trouble? What did she get?

Sister Teresa took them and read some before laying them out on the table with the others, like a suspect board.

I could read some of the words upside down, some that I had written. *I can't wait to kiss you again … I miss your warm hands on … We'll sneak out once Miss Farzana has gone to bed …*

There was nothing about our relationship that was not in the many pages in front of us.

For the first time I felt disgusted with myself. I should have never let myself get carried away with my feelings. I knew right from the start that there would be repercussions to doing this, to being this, and yet I had let myself be insanely stupid. I should have never let myself think any of this was okay. I had literally called this upon myself.

'Your mothers have been called. We will have a conversation in front of them tomorrow. You can now go back to your dorms and pack your bags. Miss Farzana, I would advise you oversee them,' Sister Teresa said, not looking at us at all.

'But Sister …' Ina tried to say something but was cut short by Sister Teresa's hand.

I had nothing to say at all.

'I don't want to hear another word from you two. You may go.'

As we walked back to the blocks, we could see girls peeping at us. Of course everyone knew by now. Rumours spread like wildfire in St Mary's, and this was not a rumour at all. In our block, the girls came out to watch the drama. I heard 'faggot' being whispered as I crossed them to go to my dorm. Even my own friends joined the others. I expected little from them, and had no one to blame but myself. No one spoke to us while we packed our bags. And the few times I tried to talk to Nitisha and Ignaz they behaved like I didn't exist. It was as if I was invisible. It hurt more than I had ever thought these things do, and all those times I had stayed silent came back to me.

At lights out, Miss Farzana stood there until I got into bed, and I heard the click of a lock after she went out. It was worse than solitary confinement, it was jail where I was the outcast. Maybe Inayat had it better. At least she didn't have friends who had disowned her in a day, as if all those years of friendship meant crap. But then, I guess it was because of her one friend that we were here.

Pema. I should have known better than to trust her.

I cried myself to sleep.

It was the same as we went for breakfast the next day. The seats next to me stayed empty. I looked up and saw that so were Inayat's.

That was our last meal at St Mary's.

By lunch our mothers had arrived and we were taken to Sister Teresa's office again.

'What has she done now,' Inayat's mother said. No wonder she didn't like her mother.

My mother, meanwhile, stood by, saying nothing at all. Which was worse, I thought. I had no idea what she was thinking. For years after Papa passed away I had been Mum's only support. I had made sure nothing ever hurt her. And then when she started working I made sure to do well all the time, made sure everything was perfect at home, hoping that she'd be so happy with me that she wouldn't go away from me as much. I remembered the time she found out about my last boyfriend and shut herself off from me. I remember how we spent the entire holiday in our own rooms, meeting only to serve ourselves food the cook left on the table. I hated disappointing her. And now I had managed to add more pain to her life than I could have ever imagined? Just for a moment of … of whatever it was. Would she leave me again and never want to come back to a daughter who was so horrible, so disgusting … and queer.

'We cannot tolerate such behaviour at St Mary's. The world may think otherwise, but we hold our ideals high and expect our students to do so too,' Sister Teresa said, passing the letters to both the mothers and the diary to Inayat's. There was silence as everyone went through the pages. Or I suppose page, because Inayat's mother read one and let go of the rest.

'Is this what I sent you away from home for, this haram!' she screamed, shoving the letters in Inayat's hands. She grabbed Inayat by the hair and slapped her across her face. And again. And again until her glasses came off. 'You're just like your father, aren't you?'

I started to bawl, but not a tear came out of Ina as her mother continued to hit her.

I could see girls collect outside of the office to get a peek at what was happening, all the noise. I turned around and saw some faces—Shefali, Rhea, Nitisha, Pema … Pema.

It lasted only a few minutes, but felt like the longest that I had ever lived.

'Are these the values I've given you, huh?' Ina's mother screamed, holding Inayat by her mouth. 'You're a curse to me. To think you have done this to me now, when I'm ... I curse the day you were born.'

'Calm down, Saba. Let's talk to her,' Amir reasoned.

'You don't tell me what to do with my daughter. She should be thrown out onto the streets, this disgrace.'

'Miss Saba, I do have to request you to calm down,' Sister Teresa said. *Now she says something*, I thought. 'This is your private matter and I would request you to handle it as such. You have been called because we feel responsible to tell you why we can no longer have your child in the school. We set a high precedent for our students and this is ... well, we condemn this behaviour.'

'You've been expelled! Look at you standing there like nothing has happened,' Inayat's mother screamed again.

'Enough,' my mother screamed. 'I have to ask you to stop. I understand that this is not okay, but I will not have you beat her up in front of me.'

So I have disappointed her.

'Yes, Saba. You must stop,' Amir said.

'Why don't you two both mind your own business,' Ina's mother snuffed.

'Miss Saba, this isn't the time and place to do this. I would request you to please sit down and sign these papers, and then I would like you and your ward to exit the school with decorum. I cannot have this be an example to the other girls,' Sister Teresa said.

'You should have paid more attention. I did not pay all that money for such loose rules,' Ina's mother continued. 'Who is the matron, I want her thrown out too!'

'Miss Saba, you will not teach me how to run my school. Not in my forty-three years have I had a case of this nature be brought to me, and I blame no one but your daughters for it. Now please do not make this more difficult than it needs to be. As it is, I have wasted two days on this repulsive matter.'

'Is there any way you could not make these papers of expulsion?' my mother interrupted. 'The girls' futures will be ruined.'

'I am sorry. A serious offense like this isn't something we take lightly, and we cannot excuse it. The best I have done is not mention the reason. I am sure you are all capable of cooking up something for the next school. Now, if you could both please sign.'

I looked up at Ina one last time as I picked up my trunk to leave. She looked back and I saw her tear up, and everything I had felt for her came rushing back even as I tried my hardest to tell my mind to shut up.

Would I ever get to see her again? Speak to her again? I thought of all the possible ways we might meet again in those few seconds before her mother slapped her again.

'How dare you look at her, you filthy girl. Do you have no shame? You really disgust me. Come now.' And she pushed her out of the door and into the girls who stood waiting. 'Yes, look at her as an example of what you mustn't do,' she said to the girls as she walked out.

'Let's go,' my mother said as she walked out after, me following silently behind. Not that there was much to be thankful for, but I was pretty grateful that my mother hadn't humiliated me like Inayat's, although I was scared about what she'd say when we were alone. If I knew her at all, she wouldn't say anything, but her shutting me out once again after what we had somewhat rebuild in the bandh would be enough.

For now though, as we drove out of the gates of St Mary's, I took a final look at what had been home for years, and I saw the girls standing outside, friends I had cared for, including Pema, and the teachers who were trying to bring them all back to class.

CHAPTER 30

PEMA

I swear I regretted it immediately. Fuck, I do every single minute still. I don't know how to live with myself. I feel so guilty all the time, and I just cannot stop replaying that day in my head. I mean, like, there was nothing I could have done to make Shefali change her mind about what I told her once I had word-vomited, I knew that. I should have also known she would tell anyone she could find about it, but I hadn't imagined she would actually go snitch to Sister Teresa to get brownie points for head girl. Of course everyone knows Sister Teresa's hatred for the queer. This one time I heard a girl came back from an outing drunk and she was only suspended for a month. Another one who was caught stealing something from Archies and brought to school by the owner got away with like three months of detention and no outings for a year. Although, let's be real, I probably should be the last person to point a finger at Shefali. Who am I to give lectures about letting people live and like doing the right thing and whatnot? I mean, honestly, if I hadn't been that insecure, wouldn't Ina and Nidra still be in school?

I had tried to keep it together for a few days right after, not think about it, pretend like everything was normal with Ina, stupidly hope that nothing would happen, but that morning when Charu told me Ina and Nidra were in Sister Teresa's office with their mothers, and when I overheard Ina's mum yelling, I couldn't hold it in me anymore.

At home Aama immediately knew something was wrong. She can always tell when I'm hiding things and it can be really annoying sometimes. Baba can never do it, although Dada can so it's not like a boy girl thing or anything. Anyways, when Aama asked me what was wrong, I couldn't do it anymore. I hugged her and broke down like a baby.

She was crazy pissed at first (for what I'd done to Ina and Nidra, not about soaking her with my tears and spit and all). She said she couldn't believe she had taught me to harm anyone, let alone my best friend. She said she was sad that I had such bitter feelings. And this time I couldn't even tell her, 'Way to hit a girl exactly where it hurts, Aama.'

But I think she could tell that I hated myself for it already. And she kind of understood why I was so insecure and angry and stuff. I'm sure she remembered all the school outings I threw a tantrum not to go on because I'd have no one to hang out with, and every time I cried because I was bored at home alone, or every birthday I told my parents I just wanted to spend with them because I had no one else to go out with. Because, for the first time, and kind of finally might I add, she asked if I wanted to change schools. 'We all learn from our mistakes, naani,' she said, giving me a hug. 'I was wrong. Now that I think about it, what happened with the girls is unfair. I don't know what Nidra and Ina feel for each other, but everyone has the right to love whoever they choose to. And you have the right to start over.' But I didn't want to. It sucked that Ina and Nidra had to leave school because of me and I got a choice to make it easier for myself. I deserved to be in St Mary's and friendless.

I kept thinking of anything I could do to help, maybe just fix a little of what I had ruined. I desperately wanted to see Ina, see Nidra, say sorry to both of them. That was the minimum. But what else? I couldn't go to Sister Teresa, not like me saying I had outed them would change the fact that she'd kicked them out for being lesbians or whatever. And we weren't living a movie where I could organize protests about it, with all the girls finally joining in and marching till Sister Teresa got thrown out.

One step at a time.

I went to Baba's study in the evening. 'Baba, can you find out where Ina and Nidra are? I wanted to meet them before they leave Darj.'

I was hoping Baba already knew everything, because honestly I was too ashamed myself to like tell anyone what I had done again. What would I even say—your daughter betrayed her best friend? Thankfully he didn't ask.

'I'll check,' he said, giving me one of those like sympathetic smiles that meant Aama had definitely spoken to him. They used to do this all the time before the agitation, and even though things were better between them, they weren't completely back to normal. *At least there's some good to come from the riots I caused*, my mind connived. Of course this made me wonder how I am like the leader of the local party. Big or small, we both had selfish reasons to do what we did and cause like total disaster around us. I just hope that unlike the agitation in town, which almost six months and one leader later still has those one-off sparks, this one dies down completely, and soon.

He came back to the table after a quick call. 'Nidra is staying at Elgin with her mother, they have a flight tomorrow morning. And Inayat is in Windamere with her parents for the day too.'

Okay, this could be my chance.

'But from what I hear, it might be better if you speak to Inayat's mother alone first,' Baba said to Aama. 'She may not let Inayat meet anyone.'

I prayed hard that wouldn't be the case. But from what I'd seen of Inayat's mother, the chances of it were pretty high.

'Aama, can I meet Nidra first?'

She nodded. I was like completely shocked that she was agreeing to everything after what I had done. But god knows parent logic. I was just grateful for it, with a whole lot more guilt.

An hour later, I was standing in the hotel lobby waiting for Nidra and like shivering even thinking about what she'd say. *What are you expecting? You bet she hates your stupid ass.* Of course my mind had to jump in when I was panicking. What was *I* supposed to say to Nidra? I know I wanted to meet her and everything, but I had no idea what I could say that would make anything better or make her hate me less.

But I found my voice as soon as I saw her, her eyes swollen like crazy, and her face all like blotchy and red and stuff. I had never seen Nidra like this. She had always looked happy, bright, brave.

'I'm sorry.'

She was angry, and hurt too. 'You ... how could ...'

People around us stopped to look as Nidra shouted at me.

'You! I still cannot believe it. I should have known. I should have never trusted you. She trusted you, blindly. And you went and did this. Forget to me, but to Inayat! She loved you, do you know that? She really cared for you. She told me you felt like family and whatnot, like a sister she never had. To think it was you. I should have known.'

'Nidra, I swear I am very sorry. I wish I hadn't. I feel ... I am so stupid.'

'No shit.'

We stood there for a minute, silent, tired and blank maybe.

'Nidra, I know you hate me, and I know I have given you a reason to and all. I also know that me saying sorry doesn't change anything. But please let me try explain. I will die if I don't tell you what happened and say sorry to you properly.'

'And why do you think you deserve a chance to live with yourself? Why shouldn't you have to suffer along with us?'

I started crying. I had been feeling exactly what she hoped I would. I knew she was right. I didn't deserve to feel better about anything I had done.

I cried until like I just couldn't anymore, and when I stopped to breathe, Nidra was holding a glass of water.

'Drink.'

I took a sip.

'Go on.'

I told her about how like Ina was the first real friend I ever had. How over the years I had never had anyone by my side until Inayat, and how I turned completely psycho and started fearing that Ina would go away too when she got close to her and everything.

'I saw the two of you that night on Lover's Road, and like just seeing how close you were made me crazy jealous. When Ina told me about you two ... you know, I don't know, I just thought ... I never cared that you guys were gay ... I didn't even think of it like that ... I just thought I was like losing her. Then in the infirmary, I just ... got so jealous again. And I told Shefali. And I swear I really regret what I did. I regretted it immediately, but there was nothing I could do to take it back. She didn't listen to me ... and then everything happened so fast.'

Nidra was sobbing now.

'I wish you had spoken to Inayat, to me,' she cried. 'Inayat truly loved you. She always said how special you were and how happy she was that she had a friend like you. Now we have honestly lost everything. My mother ... my mother hasn't spoken to me all this while. It's like she's disowned me, and I know she'll leave me again and this time never want to come back, even though I told her it was a mistake, that it would never happen again.'

'There's got to be something I can do ... I could ask Baba to speak with Sister Teresa, your mother maybe.'

'You think I would ever want to go back to that hell hole?'

'I am so sorry, Nidra. I don't know what to do. Like I feel so helpless. I feel like I should be the one who is punished. I should be thrown out, not the two of you. You two really have done nothing wrong.'

'I guess we did do something wrong. I did something wrong. I should have never done any of it.'

'No, you didn't! I mean, loving someone isn't wrong, Nidra.'

'I did, Pema. All this, it's not right. You don't understand, I can't lose my mother, she's the only family I have. I built a good life at school, Mummy and I were good too after the bandh, and I've lost all of it. You think any of it was worth it? It wasn't.'

'The world isn't the same anymore, Nidra. Even my mother, who was totally against this, agreed that everyone had the right to love whoever they choose.'

'You're lucky then I guess. As for the world, you want to think it's changed, but looks like it's just the same.'

We sat silent for some time.

'There is ... well ... can you do me a favour?' she asked, breaking the silence.

'Anything.'

'I wanted to ... could you give Inayat a letter for me? For whatever it is worth, I would like to tell her how I feel.'

'I am going to try go to her now. But you'd like trust me with it?'

'What have I got to lose?'

I mumbled an okay.

'Okay, wait here,' she said, racing up and returning with an envelope.

'I promise I won't read it,' I said, like it even mattered, even though I really wished it did.

She smiled a little.

CHAPTER 31

INAYAT

Ina,

 I don't know where to start or what to say. I've been replaying the last two days in my head and it still feels like it hasn't happened, like it just couldn't really. I go to sleep hoping it is all a dream and that we'll wake up in the graveyard and have to rush back to our dorms.
 I suppose I have to stop cooking things up and accept the truth now. I look at Mummy who isn't speaking to me beyond literally day-to-day instructions and realize that I must accept what has happened. I am so afraid she's going to leave me forever for who I am.
 We were so happy, I was so happy, and it felt like we had the shortest time together before everything came crashing down. And the weirdest part is, it happened in school. A place I have felt the safest in, I know you have too.
 Remember that night when we ran from the abandoned house, we were sitting in the graveyard and discussing what had happened, what the lady told us. She had said that in a political battle for power and money it was the innocent who were sacrificed, so many of them letting themselves be used without realizing that they were only the means to an end for some few. I don't even know if I am saying any of this correctly, but I feel like you'll get it anyways.
 That night we said that the school was our safe place or whatever. But I've been thinking, maybe all of us at school are exactly like the

people being used in the agitation. We're all told what is right and wrong. And people like you and I who fail to follow are the ones who are sacrificed so that the people in power can win, to keep their mindsets as is. Maybe the school was always just as unsafe as the outside, and we were safe only as long as we were okay to do what we were being told to, and we became dispensable when we didn't. We thought it was a win when the agitation ended and the leader went into hiding, because we got to be back together, but we forgot that there were others who were working to keep their power intact too, and they won.

I've been thinking, maybe it is better to not be on either side and just be hidden then, safe, like the old lady, and go on with life.

Speaking of hiding, Mummy has somehow managed to convince another school in Dehradun to take me mid-year. I join there in two weeks. I don't know anything else.

I don't know when we'll speak again, if we do at all, which is why I thought I should write to you at least. I felt I owed you this. I'm trying to understand what happened and what it will all mean eventually. For now I know that I don't think I have the courage to fight everyone, and more importantly fight my mother or myself for who I am. As bad as I can guess it sounds to you, I think I have decided that I would rather tell myself I don't like girls, that this was a mistake and make the best of wherever I go next. There is plenty that you and I have lost in life, so maybe you get it, but I am not ready to lose my mother or even the chance to have a normal life because I like girls, or who knows, for a short period I liked one girl.

Maybe one day I will feel differently, I don't know. Maybe the world will change and we will find each other, but, until then, please know that everything I felt for you was real, and I really wish you the best.

Yours,
Nidra

EPILOGUE

Eight months later, as Nidra sat at the pottery wheel, cutting open her fifty-third cylinder, tracing the rings on it with her fingers, pressing on the sides to find the perfect thickness, her mind wandered off to Inayat for the hundredth time. *She would have been proud of me.*

She had tried to forget about Inayat, to build a new life at St Bishop's, away from all the voices and laughs and nightmares. And she'd been successful too. Her grades were good, and she was already taking part in a lot of the school activities. There was also a possibility that she got to be captain next term. But while there had been boys who had liked her here, and some she had liked too, she couldn't get rid of how she felt for Inayat. All the promises to herself that she would not go down this path, not jeopardize her relationship with her mother who was still refusing to talk with her were faltering a little. Or perhaps it was easier now that once again she was away from it all and in the 'safety' of a new school.

But how many unanswered letters does it take for someone to stop writing? How many emails and phone calls?

As soon as Nidra had found her way around the school, she had taken every spare moment to write to Inayat, to tell her she was still thinking of her, that how she felt hadn't been for a short time at all. And every phone call started with multiple calls to her landline.

It took Nidra five months to give up, until all she was left with were questions, endless ones. *Why won't she reply? What do I do? Did Pema do something yet again to make sure Ina never writes back?*

For all the forgiveness Nidra had promised her that day at the hotel, the silence from Inayat had made her resentful of Pema, doubtful of the apologies and her intent.

'Have you heard from her?' Pema would write in every email.

And Nidra would read it and leave it unanswered. *She should suffer the same fate I have.*

But Pema continued to write to both of them, despite the silence, despite her parents begging her to forgive herself. Perhaps guilt pushes us to try to make amends for longer than one has the ability to. So she wrote, almost as if not waiting for a reply anymore.

Then, over a year later, she heard her mother come up to her room, screaming. And there it was—Inayat's handwriting on an envelope.

Dear Pema,

I know this has taken a while, but I could not have written to you without being dishonest about how I felt with regard to everything that had happened, and that would have been incorrect.

I will write properly to you soon, but for now I need you to help me find Nidra's email or address if you can. Ammi took the logins to all my old accounts so I have lost all my contacts. Luckily, I'd found one of your letters at Nani's and saved it for the day I felt strong enough to write.

I hope to hear from you soon.

Ina

P.S. I never got to thank you for getting Nidra's letter to me all those months ago. And I accept your apology. It took me a while, but I understand why you did what you did and I am sorry you felt the need to. Speak soon.

P.P.S. I've added my email on the back of the envelope. Just easier that way.

P.P.P.S You are still my best friend.

Sobbing, Pema wrote back immediately.

An hour later, Nidra's phone screen lit up with the familiar beep of an email notification.

I thought you wouldn't believe it if I simply typed out an email, so sending you a photo of my letter instead.

Nidra stared at Inayat's scrawny writing. With tears pouring down her cheeks, she read ahead.

I am sorry I haven't written to you in all these months. I want to make the excuse of Ammi having intercepted all my emails, letters, even phone calls, but that isn't it, even though factually true, not for all the while. I needed time to make sense of what happened, what I felt about it and, more importantly, your letter. In your letter you wanted to keep quiet, to disappear, to lie to yourself and the world; you said that it would be better to live a life of hiding, and that made me angry. I didn't want to hide. Even that night at the abandoned house, I wanted to run out and fight, protect the family. Hiding just did not feel right to me, not then, and definitely not with us. On our last night in Darjeeling, I remember Ammi had beaten me until every part of me ached, and yet not a single bit of me wanted to keep quiet. I was tired of writing in my diary, to my God, but I didn't want to lie or stay silent. I wanted to find a solution for myself, a way to live my truth. There was just so much I was feeling that I had to make sense of. There was guilt for what I thought my religion asked of me, what my mother expected of me, what the school demanded of us. And then there was anger at the pressure of it all, anger at being made to shun what I don't think I am capable of shunning, something that feels inherently me, something I know I didn't choose but chose me. I have spent years writing and complaining about life and not doing anything about it, but I couldn't do it any longer. And you saying that you would rather forget about that part of yourself because it would be easier, forget me too, it hurt, and I felt more alone than I ever had. I didn't understand it at all until I realized we all have our own journeys with sexuality. For even those who are straight. It is only much harder for us because we don't have enough literature, enough movies, enough support, enough anything to make us understand how we're feeling. I forgave you when I realized that I can't force you to have the same journey I have had, force you to do anything you aren't comfortable with. But it has taken me this long to make sense of it all.

I am no longer ashamed of saying I am a lesbian.

Can you believe Nani helped me navigate through all of this? Once I went back, Nana came to take me home to Hyderabad. Turns out Amir asked him to. Amir has been a real pillar, shielding me from Ammi's anger, her disdainful silence, and we've become great friends since. I felt terrible for having judged him. In all of this, in my anger at Ammi, at the school, at everything that happened, I hadn't taken a minute to see that Amir was protecting me all this while. Not until he gave me your letter that night. In the weeks that followed I sat crying in my room, feeling ashamed of telling Nani Nana what I had done, wondering if I had done wrong by my God, in pain for feeling wronged by him, and wondering how it could be wrong when it all felt so right, when it was all made by him. What would she think of me after everything she had passed down to me as teachings of God? But when I told her what had happened, who I was, who I am, she was kind. She told me that my relationship with God was sacred and not for anyone else to judge. She said it was not meant to inculcate blind fear in me, instead it should cultivate love and kindness, and a great deal of gratitude and trust while leading me on a path of good. She even said that the only way this would be wrong is if it comes with abuse, in fact the story many quote to be God's word against homosexuality is that of rape. And it has taken me some time to understand that my faith, that the tenets of it are much larger than these diktats. That there is nothing more important than honest intention and being a good human being, and that my relationship with God is mine alone, between only him and I. I wept in her arms in liberating joy, Nidra.

I read something very beautiful recently that I must share with you. It is from this book by Elif Shafak, Forty Rules of Love. I have it in front of me so I am quoting, but you must bear with me. I won't get into the details of it, but one of the rules of love that Shams talks about is this—he says, 'Nothing should stand between yourself and God. Not imams, priests, rabbis, or other custodians of moral or religious leadership. Not spiritual masters, not even your faith. Believe in your values and your rules, but never lord them over others. If you keep breaking other people's hearts, whatever religious duty you perform is no good.' There are a lot more in the book, and you must read it. It's been long since I recommended a book for you to read, but this one has taught me so much of finding my sensibilities in the middle of the noise surrounding us on what is right and wrong, what is haram and not. I hope you find your peace and path too. When I look back at our months at St Mary's and the three of us, I can't help but remember the field daisies that grew in the wild, you know the ones Pema showed us that day on Lover's Road, the one we plucked, hoping the answer on the last petal was the one we wanted? The daisy you gave me with your letter. It makes me think, perhaps all we need is time, and space, unbothered and untethered, to grow to be our own kind of beautiful.

I still have my days, days when I remember how I haven't spoken to Ammi in months (turns out she hadn't come early because she was pregnant with my baby brother and didn't feel fit to travel), but I'm not afraid of being out anymore or standing up for people who are scared to come out and forced to hide, and against those who are more willing to shun than to speak and understand. And luckily the people in my new school have been very kind. I learned this of myself during the riots, when, as afraid as I was, I wanted to do more.

I suppose this was God's plan after all. I'm no longer angry with him, and I have finally found the tawakkul Nani used to speak about. I know he is always taking care of me, even when I don't think he is.

I also found out that Abba is gay. Ammi said something about me being like Abba in school, and Amir told me about it later. All this while we thought he was having affairs, we never thought it was with a man. I've forgiven him for what he did with us and speak to him often now. He's been a great source of strength too. How unfair life must have been to him while he hid who he is for so long?

I don't know if you still feel like you want to hide, but I am hoping you don't. Because I don't know what is left of us; I would like to believe that there is enough to rebuild on, but I would like to meet you. I understand that you have your own journey to make with your sexuality, and I will never force you to do anything you don't want to, but I do think there is great liberation to be found at the end of the struggle, and I do hope you find it for yourself more than anything.

I will be in Delhi soon for a school trip and would love to see you. I am guessing you will be there too, now that school is over and you are possibly waiting for the next term.

Write back if you would like to.

Yours, Ina

Nidra stared at her screen for some time longer. It was a lot to take in, her shy Ina talking so fiercely about life. It made her smile.

She wiped her tears and hit reply.

I would love to live that liberation with you again. Damn, I sound like you. When are you here, I'll ...

She paused, staring at the cursor blink for a few seconds, pressed delete and went back to her wheel instead.

CITATIONS:

Pages 55-56:
1. Express News Service. "Mamata Banerjee: '10 Died in Post-Poll Violence, Governor Inflated Numbers.'" Indian Express, June 12, 2019. https://indianexpress.com/article/research/mamata-banerjee-darjeeling-violence-tracing-the-history-of-gorkhaland-movement-another-crisis-triggered-by-language-4698528/
2. "How a Strike Has Paralysed Life in India's Darjeeling." BBC, July 6, 2017. https://www.bbc.com/news/world-asia-india-40491066

Page 58:
1. Headlines Today Bureau. "Gorkha Leader Tamang Killed; Darjeeling Tense." India Today, May 21, 2010. https://www.indiatoday.in/india/northeast/story/gorkha-leader-tamang-killed-darjeeling-tense-74764-2010-05-20
2. NDTV Correspondent. "Gorkha League Leader Killed, Darjeeling Tense." NDTV, May 21, 2010. https://www.ndtv.com/india-news/gorkha-league-leader-killed-darjeeling-tense-418559

Page 156:
1. Shafak, Elif. "Shams." Story. In The Forty Rules of Love, 246–246. Penguin Random House UK, 2011.

ABOUT THE AUTHOR

Stuti Agarwal grew up in Darjeeling and writes books about mountains, momo and all things magic. She's the author of multiple novels, including the bestselling *The Adventures of Young Kalam*, *The Very Glum Life of Tootoolu Toop* and *#KindnessMatters*.

When she is not snuggled in her fantasy world of books, Stuti is busy being the Digital Editor at *Travel + Leisure* India & South Asia, working on her dream of a writing hut in the Cotswolds.

HarperCollins *Publishers* India

At HarperCollins India, we believe in telling the best stories and finding the widest readership for our books in every format possible. We started publishing in 1992; a great deal has changed since then, but what has remained constant is the passion with which our authors write their books, the love with which readers receive them, and the sheer joy and excitement that we as publishers feel in being a part of the publishing process.

Over the years, we've had the pleasure of publishing some of the finest writing from the subcontinent and around the world, including several award-winning titles and some of the biggest bestsellers in India's publishing history. But nothing has meant more to us than the fact that millions of people have read the books we published, and that somewhere, a book of ours might have made a difference.

As we look to the future, we go back to that one word— a word which has been a driving force for us all these years.

Read.